Later, much ~~la~~ remember her moment of truth...

Or rather, untruth. At the time, it hadn't seemed important. After all, everyone at the restaurant, except Eileen and Tom, thought she was a widow. But, right then, as Garth's steady gaze held her, she had felt trapped. Still, she barely knew him. He had told her he was staying only until December. After that, he would leave Seawood Beach. She'd never see him again. What difference did it make?

In that split second, Val justified her answer.

"My husband is dead."

"Has it been long?" was Garth's next question.

"Almost a year," she said tightly, wishing desperately she'd never come here for coffee, never gotten into this whole thing.

She didn't want to start anything with this stranger, handsome and congenial as he might be. It would just complicate her already complicated life. He seemed genuinely kind and friendly. But Val knew she couldn't allow herself the luxury of friendship. It was safer that way....

JANE PEART

was a bestselling novelist in both the secular and Christian markets, and the author of more than fifty works of suspense, historical fiction and romance.

Promises to Keep

Jane Peart

Love Inspired

Recycling programs
for this product may
not exist in your area.

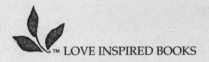 ™ LOVE INSPIRED BOOKS

ISBN-13: 978-0-373-78753-1

PROMISES TO KEEP

Printed in U.S.A.

Be strong and of good courage, do not be afraid,
nor be dismayed, for the Lord your God
is with you wherever you go.
—*Joshua* 1:9

PART I

Chapter One

It was the kind of day San Franciscans like to boast about. A brilliant postcard blue sky, the sun sparkling on the Bay where boats, their sails billowing in the crisp wind, bobbed like toys. Seated at their table in the rooftop restaurant at Ghirardelli Square, Valerie Evans and her little girl, Megan, watched the Chinese kites being flown from the marina below and floating into view. They were unaware that they were being observed with more than casual interest by a man at a nearby table.

He had noticed the child right away. About four or five years old, she was enchanting, her cherubic face haloed by a cloud of golden hair. Garth Hasten whipped out the sketchbook he always carried with him and began to draw, his pencil moving swiftly with professional skill.

"Look, Mommy," the child exclaimed, scrambling up to her knees on her chair, pointing to the colorful soaring kites. "Could I get a kite like that?"

Her mother was about to reply just as the waitress came to take their order, blocking Garth's view of the child. His pencil halted. As she studied the menu, the mother was in his direct line of vision. Quickly he turned the page and started a new sketch. She was not beautiful, not in the classic sense, the jaw too strong, the mouth too wide, but her face had an individuality that made it interesting to an artist. She had taken off her dark glasses and he saw her eyes. Under even brows, they were large, hazel maybe or gray. And there was something in them that he couldn't quite capture. Her highlighted brown hair fell from a center part curving just below her ears where tiny triangular earrings hung, glistening when she moved her head. They were her only jewelry except for a wide gold wedding band and a heavy gold link bracelet from which dangled several charms. When the waitress left, Valerie caught Garth's intense gaze. Immediately she stiffened, frowned, turned away, obviously annoyed.

He got up and walked over to their table, holding up his sketchbook so she could see his drawing of Megan. "Forgive me if I made you uncomfortable. Let me introduce myself. I'm Garth Hasten, an illustrator of children's books. Your daughter is such a lovely child I couldn't resist making a quick sketch of her."

Startled, Val glanced at the sketch. She had to admit it was very good. Professional. However, she did not like the idea of a stranger watching them like that for whatever reason. She looked away from the sketch and up to the man. Actually, he didn't look at all threatening. His expression in his tan, lean face was pleasant. There were laugh wrinkles around his very blue eyes. With his tousled thatch of graying brown hair and beard, and the Irish-knit sweater he was wearing, he gave the appearance of a roguish seafarer.

When she made no comment, Garth explained, "I'm doing a series of illustrations for a new book of fairy tales to be published by—" here he mentioned his publishers, a firm well-known for producing award-winning children's books. Seeing she recognized the name, he was encouraged and went on, "I wonder, would you be at all interested in letting your daughter model for me?" He dug into his pocket and held out his business card.

Val shook her head. "No, I'm sorry, that would be impossible."

Garth waited another minute, then said, "I understand your reluctance, but I can give you all kinds of references, professional, character, whatever. My phone number is on my card." He glanced down at Megan, who was looking from one to the other of the adults during this conversation. "It's just that this little girl would be an ideal subject."

"Mommy, it's a picture of me!" Megan exclaimed. "See, it looks just like me. Can I have it?"

Garth glanced at Val who seemed to be hesitating. He raised his eyebrows. "If your mother gives permission." He then said to Val, "I'd like her to have it." Unable to say no, Val inclined her head. Garth smiled, tore the page from his sketchbook and handed the picture to Megan. "There you go, young lady."

"Thank you," Megan said shyly.

Garth turned back to Val. "If you should change your mind, you can reach me or my rep at either of these numbers."

"Thank you, but I'm sure I won't change my mind," Val replied icily.

At that moment, the waitress appeared with their order. There was an awkward few seconds. The waitress stood waiting while Garth's hand was extended, holding out his card.

There was nothing Val could do but take it. Without reading it, she dropped it indifferently into her handbag. Deliberately, she indicated to the waitress to set down their plates.

"Sorry to have bothered you," Garth said, then went back to his table, left a tip and walked over to the cash register.

Val slipped her dark glasses back on and watched as he left the restaurant. What a strange incident, she thought, then looked fondly at her daughter. No wonder Megan had attracted the artist's eye. She was a picture. Dainty, pretty, like a doll. Except... Val sighed.

Their reason for coming into the city had not been merely for a special treat. Today they'd had an appointment with a specialist recommended by their regular pediatrician. Val turned over in her mind what Dr. Melton had told her. Megan's hearing was getting worse. Eventually, she would probably be totally deaf. It was unreal and so unfair.

Val dreaded telling Kevin the doctor's diagnosis. Kevin had an aversion to any kind of physical disability. Val remembered how he'd once told her he hated to be around people with any kind of medical disorder. "I'm just no good at it, don't ask me why. It just makes me uneasy somehow." During their marriage, Val had accepted that about him, hiding her own occasional headaches, minimizing a bad cold.

Megan's hearing loss had not been evident at first.

Some slight inattentiveness, a lack of concentration. Gradually, Val realized Megan simply could not hear unless she was spoken to directly. Then began the round of specialists. Lately, the hope they had at first began to fade.

Of course, she would have to tell Kevin even though she knew what his reaction would be. Explosive. Anger. As if it was anyone's fault.

After finishing their sandwiches and sodas, they went to a shop on the lower level that sold Chinese kites and bought one for Megan. Then they went to the parking garage where Val had left the station wagon. With Megan happily buckled in beside her, she eased down the ramp and out onto the street, then headed for the Golden Gate Bridge and the Marin suburbs.

They merged into the flow of freeway traffic and then took the Mill Valley turnoff. After making a boulevard stop, she turned at Meadowbrook, heading up a narrow winding road lined with eucalyptus trees, and drove slowly around curves up the hill. She pulled into a circular driveway just as a black Porsche backed out of the double garage. Val braked alongside.

A deeply tanned man, with stylishly groomed dark hair and neatly trimmed mustache, leaned out his open car window and, with the engine still running, asked brusquely, "Well?" Val just shook her head. Kevin's mouth tightened, but he said nothing. He stared ahead for a few seconds, then said, "I'm on my way to play racquetball at the club. I won't be home for dinner. I have a meeting tonight. I'll go in from there." He gave a small salute, shifted gears and swerved the car around, then, with a spit of gravel, roared out of the driveway.

Val sighed. She knew Kev's moods so well. Better that he bat some balls in vigorous activity than pace and prowl around the house in fury and frustration. He was tightly wound, a high-energy workaholic. She would have liked for them to be able to sit and talk quietly about Megan's prognosis. She wished she could unload some of her own anxiety. If only that was possible. But with Kevin...

Val got out of the car and held the door open for Megan. She looked up at the modern cedar-and-stone hillside house. Paid far too much for it. Had they really needed such a big, expensive house? For just the three of them, since Kevin had made it clear he considered their family complete. But he'd convinced her a good address was important.

The sound of wild barking greeted them as they started up the steps to the wraparound deck. Flynn, their huge black-and-tan Airedale came bounding down the steps from the deck. He circled them, yelping ecstatically, his tail wagging furiously, racing ahead of them, then clumsily wheeling and leaping back to be sure they were following him.

Inside, Megan called, "Harriet, we're home!"

Their weekly housekeeper, a gray-haired woman in a flowered housedress, came and stood in the archway leading from the kitchen into the hall.

"Any calls?" Val asked.

"Only Miss Grant, Mr. Evans's secretary," Harriet replied. Over Megan's head, she lifted her eyebrows inquiringly. "I s'pose there weren't any good news?"

Harriet knew about Megan's doctor's appointment. She had come to work for them when Megan was a baby and loved her dearly. Harriet had always been a rock of support to Val, who had no family of her own to lean on or confide in when the doctor first gave her the report of Megan's problem.

A faithful churchgoer, Harriet had enlisted her prayer group to pray for Megan. "We're a bunch of real prayer warriors," she'd told Val, assuring her they had added Megan's healing to her list of heavenly requests.

"'Fraid not." Val sighed. "By the way, Mr. Evans won't be home for dinner. So since it'll just be Megan and me, you might as well leave early, Harriet."

Val picked up the mail on the hall table and carried it with her into the living room. Walled with windows, it had a spectacular view of the hills, which were beginning to show the first gold and bronze tinges of autumn color.

Slipping her feet out of her leather flats, Val curled up in a corner of the curved coffee-colored sectional sofa. There was nothing much in the mail. She started to sift through the few envelopes. Mostly ads, two catalogs. Kevin must have already gone through it, taken the important stuff. She put the rest on the coffee table, then leaned her head back against the velour cushions. It had been a long day and a discouraging one. If only she had someone to talk to about Megan. Even if Kevin were here, he wouldn't have wanted to talk about it. He would probably have shut himself up in his den with the work he always seemed to bring home.

Val closed her eyes, rubbing her temples that were beginning to throb. This was not the first night recently that Kevin hadn't been home for dinner. He hadn't said anything at breakfast about having to go back to the

bank. In fact, he had planned to take the whole afternoon off and play racquetball. Something must have
come up. Harriet said his secretary had called.

Megan wandered into the room, followed by Flynn.
She went over to the bookcase where her games and toys
were kept on a lower shelf, got out one of her puzzles.
She plopped down on the rug, emptied out the pieces
and began to work on it. Flynn stretched out beside her,
his big head and paws as close to her as possible, his
eyes slavishly adoring.

Soon Harriet, in her coat and wearing an incredible
purple knitted hat, appeared at the living-room arch.
"Well, I'm on my way."

"Good night, Harriet, we'll see you on Thursday."
Val smiled.

"Night, Harriet!" Megan chirped.

"Good night, sweetness." Harriet blew her a kiss.

A few minutes later, they heard the chugging sound
of Harriet's old sedan's engine reluctantly start, followed by a grinding shift of gears as she went out the
driveway and down the hill.

The house was quiet, peaceful. Again Val wished
Kev was home. It had been a long time since the three
of them had had dinner as a family or spent the evening together.

The sky began to blaze. The oncoming sunset sent a
brilliant light into the room. It fell on Megan, who was
all concentration as she fitted the pieces of her puzzle together, turning her light hair into golden satin.
She was such a pretty child and so dear. Val wished
Kev would spend more time with her. Val frowned.
Kev worked too hard. He was so ambitious, so eager

to move up the corporate ladder. But other things were important, too. She wished she could make him see that. Megan was important, especially now. They would soon have to talk about how they could best help her if, as the doctor predicted, her hearing loss became more severe. Make some decisions about her schooling, her future. Yes, she and Kevin must talk about it.

They never seemed to have a chance to talk about things. Kev seemed to have so many evening meetings after banking business hours. Unwanted, a nagging thought intruded. Had it just been since Rhonda became his secretary that Kevin had started working later and later?

An image of Rhonda came vividly. Val had met her for the first time a few months ago. She had stopped by the bank because she and Kev were going to lunch and then pick out birthday presents for Megan. Rhonda was undeniably attractive, tall, masses of auburn hair, a good figure that her knitted dress showed off to advantage. She'd been very pleasant to Val, effusive, actually. Seated as she was at the entrance to the loan officers' desks, Rhonda would make a good impression on the bank's customers.

Val quickly thrust back her stab of suspicion. How silly to imagine Rhonda had anything to do with Kev's frequently being late. Kev explained that a great deal of the bank's business was done outside the bank, after hours. This sometimes necessitated meeting a potential client or bank customer after work. "It's a good idea for them to see you in a different setting. Get to know you on a more personal level."

Still, Val didn't like it. Life should have definite compartments. There should be a better balance between work and family. She wished Kev felt that way. Moving up the corporate ladder was the most important thing to him. "Later, when I've really made it. There'll be plenty of time." This was his argument whenever Val brought up the subject. But time was quickly going by. Megan's childhood was going quickly, too....

"All done!" Megan exclaimed. "See, Mommy, got it all put together. Isn't it nice?"

"Yes, darling, very nice. Ready to have supper?" Val uncurled herself from the sofa and stood, searching with one foot for her shoe. "Are you hungry? Since Daddy isn't coming, we'll just eat in the kitchen, okay?"

"Is he going to Rhonda's?" Megan asked.

Astonished at the question, Val halted, one shoe on, the other dangling. "Rhonda? How do you know Rhonda, honey?" As well as she could recall, there hadn't been any occasion where the little girl might have met Kevin's secretary.

"With Daddy."

"Oh, did Daddy take you by his office?" Val asked. A few days ago, she'd had a dental appointment and Kev had volunteered to pick Megan up at play school where she went three days a week.

"No, on Saturday."

"Saturday?"

"You know, Saturday, when you went out with Emily."

Val remembered that Kevin had reluctantly agreed to take Megan to the park when the sitter had canceled at the last minute. "Oh?" Val waited, then asked, "So where did you see Rhonda?"

"We went to Rhonda's 'partment. It has a swimming pool. We sat on her balcony. We could see people swimming. But I didn't have my bathing suit."

Why hadn't Kevin mentioned taking Megan to his secretary's apartment? Unless it wasn't important. Or maybe it was too important. Either way, it bothered her. She glanced at Megan. She wanted to ask her more, but she wasn't going to pump their child about it. But she didn't like it. She didn't like it at all. She intended to ask Kev about it. There was probably some simple explanation.

But Val didn't have the chance. Something much more serious happened. She waited up until ten. Then she took a bath, got into bed and read until midnight. Kevin still hadn't come home. At one, her eyes drooping, having read the same sentence over several times, Val turned out the light and went to sleep.

She was never sure what awakened her. But she sat up suddenly, fully awake. She sensed rather than heard movement in the house. Aware that Kevin must have come in, Val reached for her robe, thrust her feet into slippers and went down the hall to the living room.

Kevin was sitting on the sofa, his head lowered, holding a half-empty glass of amber fluid in a glass, a bottle of whiskey on the coffee table in front of him. As Val walked in, he raised his head, turned and looked at her. Immediately, she knew something was terribly wrong.

His face was ashen under the tan, giving him a haunted look. Staring at her from deep hollows, his eyes were full of fear. For a moment, Val couldn't find her voice. Her throat felt tight and sore. She couldn't seem to draw a breath. Finally, she managed to ask, "Kev, what is it? What's happened."

He took a long swallow of the liquid in the glass, draining it, then gave a hoarse laugh. "I'm finished. It's all over."

"What do you mean?" Val moved toward him, feeling she was treading on quicksand. "What do you mean?"

He lifted the bottle and poured another few inches into his glass, then held it up as if studying it. "I've blown it, that's what. Embezzled. Hundreds of thousands in bogus loans. I was going to put it back, every last cent of it, if I'd only had a little more time." He took a quick sip, shook his head. "Time, that's all I needed. But the bank examiners arrived." He laughed harshly. It sounded more like a grunt or a groan. "They never give any advance notice. I just got word that they were there... Well, it's too late now."

Her knees began to tremble, grow weak. She sat down at the end of the sofa and began to shiver. Long, deep shudders shook her body.

It was the beginning of a nightmare, one from which she couldn't wake up. It was the beginning of a whole new chapter of her life, and the end of another.

Chapter Two

Val felt as if she were sleepwalking as she entered the courtroom. She took a seat in the front row of the spectator section behind the table where Kevin's lawyer, Brad Hensley, was going over some papers. He turned, briefly acknowledged her with a nod, then went back to whatever he was reading.

This was it, Val thought. This was what they had finally come to after all these nightmarish weeks. Kev had refused to have a trial. He thought his chances would be better if he pleaded guilty and threw himself on the mercy of the court. He felt sure if he declared his remorse and assured the judge of his firm intention of repaying every cent of the money, saying that he had never intended to keep any of it, that he had used it to take care of the temporary shortfall from some unwise investments, he'd most likely get a suspended sentence and probation.

That was his story. Val wasn't sure Brad believed him, but that's the way he had presented Kev's case to the judge. And today he would be sentenced.

Kev was so sure his own sales skills would work in

court the way they had worked in most areas of his life up until now. To Val, it seemed total madness not to call character witnesses, former employers, fellow workers who could vouch for him, provide some defense. But, as usual, she had been unable to talk Kevin out of anything he had decided to do.

At least there'd be no jury filing in, giving her, the wife of the defendant, curious looks. Suspicious ones, too, probably thinking she must have known what her husband was doing.

Val stiffened. The adage, "tarred with the same brush" came to mind. She had already felt the scorn and heard the whispers of their neighbors. She had little pride left to hang on to now. She smoothed the skirt of her blue suit, ran her fingers along the braid trim of the jacket. She'd purposely worn this outfit. Blue was Kevin's favorite color; that's why she had chosen it this morning. Nervously, she touched her hair. Kevin liked her naturally light brown hair highlighted, so she'd had it done the day before. Although she certainly couldn't afford it.

Actually, she couldn't afford much of anything anymore. After Kevin's arrest, their checking and savings accounts had been impounded. Creditors had lost no time repossessing all their belongings: furniture, Kev's elaborate exercise equipment, golf clubs, TVs, cars. The house, of course, which Val discovered Kevin had mortgaged to the hilt in a desperate effort to recoup some of his losses, went with everything else. Nothing was left that she could sell for cash. Not that she would have wanted anything that had been purchased with the money Kevin embezzled, she thought bitterly.

While Kev was in the county jail awaiting his trial, Val had lived on the small insurance policy her parents had left her. But that was almost gone. The only other money available was a few hundred dollars in traveler's checks from one of their last trips she had never cashed. And those wouldn't last long.

When a door at the side of the courtroom opened and a police officer brought Kevin in, all thoughts of herself vanished. The look on Kev's face struck Val to the very heart. He had a terrible set expression. His eyes looked empty. His glance in her direction merely grazed her and he turned quickly away. She had hoped to send him signals of support, but there was no chance. He took his place beside Brad and the two murmured together for a few minutes before the bailiff announced in a loud voice, "All rise," and the judge entered.

Afterward, Val remembered little else other than the judge's deep voice asking, "How does the defendant plead?" then Kevin's answer, "Guilty." She had then expected Kevin to launch into his own defense. But it didn't happen. Had Brad persuaded him otherwise or had the die already been cast? All she clearly recalled were the words "seven to fifteen years." She felt her whole body sway as if from a severe blow, then her knees sagged and she had to grab onto the railing in front of her to steady herself. A wave of nausea left her weak and dizzy.

Slowly the reality of the sentence hit her. If Kevin served the full term, he would be forty-seven, she would be forty-five, and they would be middle-aged, half their lives gone. Megan would be a grown woman!

Val was to be allowed fifteen minutes with Kevin

before he was taken away, driven upstate to the prison where he would be spending the next years of his life. Dazedly, she walked out into the lobby. Out of the corner of her eye, she thought she saw Mr. Carson, Kev's immediate boss at the bank. If he saw her, he pretended not to, quickly averting his head. He must have caught some of the flak when the discrepancies and false accounts came to light in his department, "on his watch." Ironically, Val recalled his former jovial demeanor, the hearty greetings that were usual when they met at some bank party or other social function. He had always declared loudly and often to any and everyone that "they were all a big family." He'd clap an arm around Kev's shoulders and tell her heartily, "This is my boy. We have great plans for Kevin, Mrs. Evans. He's our shining star." Now, he wouldn't even meet her gaze.

"This way, ma'am," a bailiff said, beckoning her.

Before she could follow, Brad Hensley approached. Stiffly, he thrust a manila folder at her. "There are some documents in here you'll need to look over, Val. If there's anything you don't understand, you can call my office. However, I believe it's all self-explanatory." He looked so uncomfortable, Val almost felt sorry for him. He mumbled something that sounded like, "Really sorry about this, Val." Then he turned and made a quick exit out the courthouse door.

Glad to be rid of us, Val thought. Not that she blamed him. Who wanted to be seen associating with a thief, or even the wife of one? She felt sure some people suspected she had known what Kev was doing. Spent the money herself.

The bailiff was holding open the door to a room down the hall for her. She hurried toward it.

Kevin was standing with his back to the door, staring out the barred window of the small, bare room into which she was ushered. He turned at her entrance and her first impulse was to go into his arms. But he hadn't opened them. In fact, he stood rigidly, his arms close to his sides. His glance went over her head and she realized a guard would remain during their last meeting.

"Kev," she said, her voice cracking a little as she went toward him. But as her arms went around him, she felt him stiffen.

He moved out of her embrace, then took her by the wrists. His expression was grim. "Listen, Val, there's not much time and I have some important things to say."

His intensity frightened her. His brusqueness hurt her. But maybe he was afraid to show any emotion, afraid to look weak. Kev was always conscious of his impression on other people. Even an officer of the court.

"Do you understand? There are things I want you to promise."

She nodded, knowing at this point she would have promised him anything. Anything that might somehow take the desperation out of his eyes. But she was unprepared for what he demanded.

"First, you've got to divorce me."

"Kev, you can't mean that!"

"I've never meant anything more. Next, you've got to take Megan and move somewhere away from here, even out of the state, if possible. Change your name. You've got to start a new life for the two of you where no one knows you and no one can connect you with me. Understand?"

"But, Kevin…" His fingers gripped more tightly, hurting her slender wrists. "I don't want to divorce you, Kev. This isn't a life sentence—"

"It might as well be."

"But you may not even have to serve the whole term. There's good behavior—no prior record—"

"Look, Val, believe me, I know. I've discussed this with Brad. There's a whole big political thing involved in the justice system right now. White-collar crime, they call it. Don't let them get away with it. This judge is up for election. If nothing else, he wants to make an example of me. This is a high-profile case in his district. So I'm not going to get any breaks." Val's wrists began to throb from the way he was gripping them. "Well, do I have your promise?"

Tears came stinging into her eyes. "Oh, Kev, please don't ask me to do this. When you get out, we can—"

"Haven't you heard anything I've said?" Kevin interrupted her. "Do what I say." He let go her hands and flung her away from him, then took a few steps toward the door where the guard stood impassively.

"Wait, Kev." Val caught his arm, "Yes, of course I'll do whatever you want. Please, don't be angry."

He half turned back. "Promise?"

She nodded, her throat too constricted to speak.

"Okay, then. Remember it's got to be a complete break. I don't want Megan growing up with a con for a father." His voice rasped.

Val knew he was fighting his own emotions. She went over to him, put her arms around his neck and clung to him, tears streaming down her face. Over Kevin's shoulders, she saw even the guard looked distressed. It struck her that in spite of having to perform their duty, these people were human. No matter how many similar scenes they must have witnessed, they could feel the pain of such partings.

Kevin's hands pried her clasped fingers loose and he pushed her away. To the guard, he said, "I'm out of here. Let's go." Val was sobbing now. She pressed both her hands against her mouth as she watched Kevin leave with the deputy.

This couldn't be happening, Val screamed silently. But it was. That truth finally hit her. She slumped into one of the wooden chairs, weeping uncontrollably.

Chapter Three

Val woke up as the gray light of dawn filtered through the slats of the venetian blinds. Struggling out of the grogginess of exhausted sleep into which she'd fallen, she raised herself on her elbows and looked around the unfamiliar room.

At first, she couldn't figure out where she was. Then she remembered and came fully awake. The shock of what had happened yesterday brought it all back. She closed her eyes as if to block out the horror. But it was impossible. A deep shudder went through her. There was no escape. The events of the day before took shape in her mind. After she left the courthouse, she'd booked a room at a downtown hotel, then gone to pick up Megan at Harriet's house.

Megan had stayed with Harriet for a few days before Kevin's court appearance. She had kept Flynn, too. Harriet's husband was a disabled vet, confined to a wheelchair, and when Val wondered what they would do about the dog after they left Meadowbrook, Harriet had offered to keep him. "He's been company for Lew," she told Val. "He's here by himself most days when I'm out working. He's really taken to him."

Flynn was just one more thing that had to go. Val was doubtful if she could find a place to live with a child, much less a dog. A dog as large and as used to having room to run as Flynn. She had already made phone calls about rentals and discovered that children and dogs were liabilities for most places she could afford.

Val wasn't even sure what that was. She had to find some kind of job. And soon. She would have to support herself and Megan. But how? She hadn't worked since before Megan's birth. And then only as a saleswoman in a gift shop boutique. What did she have to offer a prospective employer? Val was grateful to Harriet. It made Megan's parting with Flynn easier knowing Harriet would take care of him.

Val pulled on her robe, slid her feet into slippers, fighting desperately the sense of desperation that threatened to overwhelm her. At the window, she peered through the slats of the blind. Just across the square stood the brick courthouse. She shuddered and turned away from the view. Her gaze went to Megan.

The little girl was still asleep, hair spread tangled on the pillow, rosebud mouth partly opened, plump cheeks resting on dimpled hands. She seemed untouched by all they had been through. Thank God she was free from all Val's anguish and anxiety. Completely trusting that her mother would take care of her. Little did she know the panic with which Val awakened, the fear that had been Val's constant companion for the past weeks.

Megan thought everything was an adventure. Even when Val had told her they were moving. She helped pack up her toys, books and games to be put in storage until they knew where they would be living, what they were going to do. It was then that she had showed Val the sketch the artist had made of her. That day they had been in the city at the rooftop restaurant in Ghirardelli Square seemed so long ago. Val had almost forgotten about it in the wake of all that had happened since. In fact, it was that very night that Kev had told her about the embezzlement. She had not had the slightest premonition that afternoon that their world was going to come crashing down around them.

There were so many things to decide, so much to face.

What did she do now? Where did she go from here? For the first time, she really confronted the question of what her next step would be. Somehow she had lived on the false hope that Kevin might receive a short jail term, even a suspended sentence, but now she knew that wasn't going to happen. There was no one to tell her what to do.

She took out the file folder Brad Hensley had thrust into her numb hands. Brad's demeanor had been cold, businesslike. It was hard to remember he had once been a friend. His whole attitude toward her had changed. As if he thought what had happened to them was contagious and he wanted to avoid contact. Yesterday she had been too upset to look inside the folder to see what he was talking about. Her mind had been on Kevin, the sentence the judge had just handed down. Far stiffer than Brad had led them to believe. If Brad had really worked for Kevin, would her husband have received less than the maximum in a state penitentiary?

Well, it was over now. No appeal of the sentence was possible.

With shaky hands, Val opened the folder. Divorce papers were the first thing she saw. So Brad had been in on this decision, as well. She shuddered. No matter what she had promised Kevin, this seemed a horrible solution to their problems. She put it aside and went on to the other legal papers on which her signature was needed.

What were her two most pressing needs? A place to live and a job? Slowly, Val began to understand why Kevin wanted her to change her name, to take Megan and move as far away as she could from this small community where they were known. Kevin's conviction had made the papers. If she applied for a job with Kevin's last name, prospective employers might identify her as his wife. Maybe they'd even think of her as an accomplice who'd lived on stolen money! And who could she give as a character reference?

For the first time, the awful reality of her situation struck Val. When the court had sentenced Kevin, it had sentenced her, as well.

A feeling of despair swept over her. She looked around the drab, impersonal room. Anonymous, she thought, that's what we have to become. Her gaze landed on their suitcases, which she had just dumped at the door the night before, not even bothering to unpack anything but Megan's nightie and her own, their toothbrushes and toothpaste. Until she figured out what to do, they would have to stay here.

Wearily, she opened the biggest suitcase and took out some of the things to place in the dresser. As she opened the top drawer, she saw the Gideon Bible. It surprised her until she recalled she had heard of the organization whose main ministry was placing a Bible in hotel and motel rooms. At the same time, she felt a pang of guilt. In all this terrible time, she had prayed only desperate prayers. Prayers without any real sense of direction, just tortured cries for help, wrung out of a bewildered mind, a broken heart. But she hadn't even felt help would be forthcoming. They were in trouble. Big time. But she had no real faith they would be rescued. "You reap what you sow" was the kind of phrase that came to her. Kevin had sowed a lot of bad seeds and they were reaping them. Even as the truth of that came to her, it was no comfort.

Val took out the Bible. Her grandmother, she recalled, had always said the answers to life were in the Bible. If they were, Val knew she needed some answers now. She opened it, turning the pages randomly. Was there some direction, some guidance for her within this ancient book? Something for now? Some of the Psalms were familiar, but as Val's eyes searched them, nothing seemed relevant. She came to Proverbs and as she turned the pages her gaze stopped at Chapter 3, Verse 5. "Trust in the Lord with all your heart, And lean not on your own understanding; In all your ways acknowledge Him, And He will direct your paths."

That made sense. Val felt somewhat apologetic. Why would God even want to listen to her prayers? Although she had always gone to Sunday school as a child and, until she met Kevin, attended her church's youth group, it had been a long time since she had sought Him. After Megan was born, she had often suggested to Kevin that they find a church to go to as a family. But Kevin had not been interested and she had not pursued it. As usual, it was easier to go along with Kev than confront him. Another thing for which she blamed herself. In a way, it seemed hypocritical to come to God now that she was in such desperate circumstances.

Still, what other resource did she have? Holding tight to the book, Val closed her eyes and prayed, *"Dear God, I need direction. I don't know what to do, where to go. Unless You show me, I am at a loss. Please help me. I promise I'll always be grateful."* It seemed an inadequate prayer, but it was the only thing she could think of to do.

Megan stirred in her sleep and Val put the Bible back in the drawer. When Megan woke up, they got dressed and went down to the coffee shop. The little girl skipped along beside her, swinging Val's hand. She was happy about all the exciting new things they were doing, like sleeping in a hotel, eating breakfast out.

On a nearby table someone had left a morning paper and Val picked it up. While Megan happily drowned her pancakes in syrup, Val glanced through the want ads not knowing quite what she was looking for. The paper covered a wide area and jobs were advertised in many of the smaller towns in the southern part of the state. Suddenly, a name seemed to jump out at Val, one that instantly brought back memories. Seawood. "Popular restaurant, formerly Le Chalet, under new ownership, now hiring waitresses for the coming season."

Seawood was a small town halfway between San Francisco and Carmel, a picturesque resort about a hundred miles down the coast. Years ago when Megan was a baby, Kevin had come home one day driving a shiny

British sports car. With a broad wink, he told her he was test-driving it. At least that's what he had told the dealer. "Come on, honey, let's go." Although Val hadn't thought it quite honest to pretend to the salesman that he was thinking of buying it, Kevin had shrugged off any protests. "Who knows, but someday we'll be buying one like this. Anyway, why pass up a chance to drive a sweet number like this with a ten-thousand-dollar engine?" He grinned. That grin of his usually melted her resistance to any of Kevin's ideas. Persuaded, Val hastily called her regular sitter and they took off. To Carmel.

It had been a glorious day and they had driven, top down, along a beautiful span of scenic highway, on one side towering hills dark with Monterey pines and on the other, the ocean exploding dramatically against the rocky cliffs.

They'd had dinner at Le Chalet, a French restaurant whose menu Val couldn't read and whose prices she didn't dare look at too closely. Kevin had ordered a gourmet meal with an assurance that even then amazed Val. Before their dessert came, Kevin excused himself. When he came back to the table, he placed a key beside Val's plate. "Guess what? We're staying over." He held up a hand as Val opened her mouth to ask about Megan. He'd called the sitter, made arrangements for her to spend the night.

The fairy-tale cottage was reached by climbing a path up a wooded hillside behind the restaurant. It seemed to cling to the rocks high above the ocean. There was a fireplace and a canopy bed. Kevin had ordered another bottle of wine and they sipped it while sitting on the little balcony. Val worried what this would do to their budget, but Kevin wouldn't let her even guess.

"Just think of it as a second honeymoon, babe." That was always Kevin's excuse for any impulsive weekend trip or unplanned vacation. Their life together had been a series of second honeymoons, Val thought ruefully. The trouble was they'd never settled down to a real marriage.

Val remembered that time with a mixture of nostalgia and regret. Maybe she should have protested his extravagances more. Especially when they couldn't possibly afford it. Like that weekend.

She really had to take some of the blame for the way they had lived. She had always wanted to please him, but why? Because she was afraid of his sudden shifts of mood, his temper. It was much easier, pleasanter, to go along.

Val's attention went back to the Help Wanted ad.

"Now hiring for the coming season: attractive, personable young ladies as waitresses for restaurant in small coastal community. Top wages, pleasant working conditions, good benefits. For interview contact Manager, Eileen McDermott." A post-office box and phone number was given. "Seawood, CA."

Val read the ad over again. Maybe seeing this ad was some kind of sign. Maybe it was God's way of providing for her and Megan. Of course, she wasn't an experienced waitress, but they had not prefaced the job as requiring experience. Val had worked in an ice-cream parlor part-time when in high school. Not the kind of job to qualify her for one in a large, busy restaurant. Still, she had the feeling that she ought to follow her hunch.

Or, maybe, this was the answer to her prayer? "Trust in the Lord…and He will direct your paths." Maybe He was directing her path. She needed to find a job and a place to live. And right away. They couldn't stay in the hotel indefinitely. She had to make a move. One step at a time, they always said. Well, she'd take that step, Val decided, tearing out the ad.

After returning with Megan to their room, she sat at the phone and dialed the number.

A pleasant-sounding woman's voice answered, identifying herself as Eileen McDermott. Val asked if there were still openings for waitresses and was told yes. An interview was set for ten the following morning. "And what did you say your name was?" Mrs. McDermott asked.

For a moment, Val was caught, then she swallowed hard. "Valerie, Valerie—" a slight hesitation "—Madison." That was the first time she'd used her maiden name in years.

Val's hand holding the phone felt clammy with nervousness. She took a long, dragging sigh. She hated any kind of lying. She was just following Kev's orders.

Val quickly packed up their things. She didn't give herself a chance for second thoughts, knowing doubts could creep in and she might change her mind. The next step was the bus station where she purchased tickets to Seawood. An underlying excitement had taken the place of the uncertainty. The woman on the phone had sounded very nice. Perhaps Val could convince her to take a chance, despite her inexperience. She was scared, but at least she'd made a decision.

As the two of them settled into their cushioned seats

in the bus, the huge vehicle rolled out of the terminal and lumbered toward the freeway. This was another new experience for Megan, who pressed her snub nose to the window and bounced up and down. They were on their way to a new life, whatever that was. Val had one bad moment when she spotted the sign, Mill Valley Next Exit. How often had she taken that turnoff. That was the past, that was over, she reminded herself as she watched the sign slide past as the bus roared along the freeway.

They'd been so happy when they first moved to that house. Kevin's enthusiasm had soon overcome Val's initial resistance to its location, size and all the new furniture. Even the hiring of Harriet to houseclean had seemed an unnecessary expense. But Kev had insisted. "We're moving up, babe." The promotion to new accounts at the bank had just come through and his future had looked very bright. In fact as he was fond of singing to her, whenever she protested, "Everything's coming up roses." And it did seem that way. Only Val didn't know it was on borrowed time and that time would soon run out.

And she had to admit they had been happy there for three, almost four years—until Kevin's arrest and the resulting shock waves that reverberated through their affluent neighborhood. Overnight they became anathema to their friends and neighbors. They'd quite pointedly turned the other way if she happened to see them in the small shopping center. After that the phone never rang, except for a few crank calls—until she had the number changed. No one ever came by or dropped in. It was as though suddenly she'd ceased to exist. Val knew they would all be relieved, the sooner she was gone the better. The morning of Kev's court date when she left the house for the last time, she'd stood at the end of the driveway, waiting for a cab. Val was sure she could almost feel hostile eyes boring into her.

It had all been so different before. The friendly get-togethers, the sharing of child care and carpooling, helping each other give kids' birthday parties, the backyard barbecues, the Sunday brunches on someone's flower-bordered patio. They'd been part of the upwardly mobile young marrieds. Now, they'd become invisible to everyone. The morning of the sentencing, Val had left Megan with Harriet, who was the only one who had stood by them all these weeks. In the old days, before anything had happened, it would have been natural for Val's next-door neighbor, Emily, to keep Megan. But she had not spoken to Val since the news broke.

Val felt a tug on her sleeve as Megan asked a question, and glad to pull her mind back to the present, she answered it. Megan kept chattering and pointing out things as they traveled. It was a welcome diversion for Val and kept her from dwelling on their hazy future. After a while, Megan got tired. Val pushed up the armrest and Megan put her head on her lap and curled up on the seat. As she smoothed the child's silky hair, Val wondered how tomorrow's interview would go.

Finally, the bus stopped in Seawood. Val got their luggage and went into the small station. At the snack bar, Val ordered a couple of hamburgers and then checked into the small motel across the street. The room was spare but clean and had a small black-and-white TV. After Megan fell asleep, Val took a shower, shampooed her hair. As she set it, she surveyed herself in the bathroom mirror. What she'd been going through in recent months plainly showed. She had lost weight and there were what seemed to be permanent circles under her eyes. Makeup would help. She just hoped she could manage to look "attractive, personable and young" enough to be hired as a waitress at the restaurant now renamed The Seawinds.

The next morning, Val found out from the motel manager that the restaurant was located about three miles away. Too far to walk from the center of town. So after they ate breakfast, Val hailed a taxi. When she gave the driver her destination, he remarked that it was one of the "classiest" places in the resort town. "The new owners redecorated, renovated it to a fare-thee-well. Course everything's kinda slow right now, but when the season opens I bet it'll be popular. People don't mind driving someplace they know they'll get good food and the atmosphere's right."

"I'm hoping to get a waitress job there," Val volunteered.

"That a fact? I've heard the McDermotts are nice folks to work for," he said as he pulled to a stop in front of a rambling, low-roofed rustic building built on a projectory with a sweeping view of the ocean. As he leaned back over the front seat to open the rear door he said, "Well, good luck."

I'll need more than luck, Val thought, whispering a prayer. If she wasn't hired, this trip would have been for nothing. She was sure this little town did not have that many other job opportunities.

Mrs. McDermott, an attractive woman in her late forties, with prematurely silver hair, greeted Val warmly. Her genuine, friendly manner put Val at ease right away. She gave Megan a cup of cocoa while she poured two cups of coffee for them. She opened the interview casually by telling Val that she and her husband had owned a number of restaurants, the last one in San Francisco. But it had been a hectic pace and they'd decided they wanted a less stressful life. So when they heard that this restaurant, closed for a few seasons, had come on the market, they'd bought it and moved to Seawood.

"We're pretty laid-back." She laughed. "That's why we're only open five days a week and then only for dinner. My husband loves to fish, so this gives him plenty of time. I stay busy managing the restaurant. Now, tell me about yourself," she invited Val with a smile.

As truthfully as she dared, Val told her she was raising her daughter on her own, that she hadn't had much recent experience as a waitress but was more than willing to work hard and learn.

"Well, I don't see why you wouldn't work out just fine. You're pretty and smart and the work isn't too difficult. You'll have plenty of chances to get the hang of it. We have an orientation week for new employees before we open, which isn't until after Memorial Day. Then we expect to swing into our busy season right up until Labor Day. By that time you'll be experienced." She laughed.

Just then, the front door opened and a tall, gray-haired man walked inside. Mrs. McDermott's face lit up. "Oh, here's my husband."

The man was casually dressed in a plaid flannel shirt and blue jeans, and his weathered face was deeply lined.

He had a wide smile and twinkling blue eyes. He spotted Megan immediately. "Well, hello, little lady, who are you?"

"I'm Megan." She looked up at him with a dimpled smile.

"Tom," Mrs. McDermott called, "come over here. I'd like you to meet one of our new waitresses, Valerie Madison."

Val almost said Evans automatically to correct her, then caught herself in time.

"Hello, nice to meet you. Does that little charmer belong to you?"

"Yes, that's Valerie's daughter." Mrs. McDermott turned to Val. "Tom adores children. We have two grandsons, but they live back east so we don't get to see them often or have much chance to spoil them." She handed Valerie a printed application. "This is merely a formality. Just need your Social Security number, that sort of thing."

"Then I have the job?" Val asked.

"Yes, of course, and since you just got into town, you're looking for a place to live, right?"

Val nodded, amazed at how things were falling into place. "Yes, I'm staying at the motel in town, but—"

Mrs. McDermott smiled. "Let me pull a few strings." And she picked up the phone. After some banter with the person on the other end, Val heard her ask, "Are you still renting those cottages out on the far end of Beach Road? Good. I've got a renter for you." After she hung up, she wrote something down on a slip of paper and handed it to Val. "They're not fancy," she said. "Just basic. It's a part of the town that never developed. The developers ran into some problems with the coastal planners or something and Bob bought up all the cottages for back taxes. Got them for a song and rents them cheap. Anyway, being off-season, the rent will be even cheaper. Bob will probably give you a deal. He'll be happy to get one off his hands. Something he doesn't have to worry about. Much better to have a place occupied. And it's walking distance to here and to some small shops, the post office, grocery."

Val thanked her. "You've been very kind."

"We're glad to have you on board," Mrs. McDermott told her.

When Val went outside with Megan, she was surprised to find the taxi still there. The driver was reading the newspaper behind the wheel.

"Got the job, did you? Thought so."

With a start, Val realized Seawood was a small town. And like in any small town, nothing much went unnoticed. She would have to be extra careful about what she said and who she said it to if she was going to protect Megan and herself from being identified.

"Where to now, miss?" the driver asked, folding his newspaper, then holding open the rear door for them.

She told him about the rental and he took her right to the Dobbs Realty office. It had been a long time since anyone had been as friendly and helpful as this man and the McDermotts. Even so, Val warned herself she still had to be cautious.

The driver told her that he'd wait.

"You're sure?"

"Yep, haven't got another fare anyway."

After Val left the office, the same taxi drove them to

the motel to collect their bags and then out to the cottage she had just rented. The driver kept up a running monologue all the way, telling her the same story as Mrs. McDermott had with more embellishments about the "hotshot" developers who had bought the property ten years ago, hoping to make a "quick buck" but who then had dropped the whole project.

Mentally, Val winced. This could well be the ill-fated investment Kevin had been enthusiastic about. But like so many of his other schemes, it had petered out. It seemed a strange coincidence. But then lately, her life was filled with a series of unexpected incidents.

"Them cottages are not up to code, did Bob tell you that?" the driver asked. "No heating, no electricity? Couldn't pass the state building laws. Bob probably told you they were built for summer rentals. The season is short here on this coast, but as I said, it just never took off. But you'll be okay. Most of the year we don't get too much cold weather, and they have stoves—wood-burning ones. Think you can manage?" He looked at Val in his rearview mirror, raising bushy eyebrows.

She nodded, praying she could. The Realtor had told her the same thing, so when she bought groceries, she had also purchased kerosene for the lamps that were in the cottage and a box of Presto-logs for the stove. What neither Bob nor the taxi driver nor the grocery clerk knew was that whatever the conditions were she had to manage. At that kind of rent, somehow she would. The two months rent she had to pay in advance left her just barely enough to get by until she started working. She'd been lucky today. She had a job and a place to live. That was more than she'd had yesterday.

The cab turned off the main road onto a rutted one that dipped down parallel to the ocean. Five small, gray frame houses with slanted roofs, widely spaced from each other, were the only buildings in sight. The taxi braked to a jolting stop in front of the first one, a weathered shingled cottage. There was a badly listing fence with a sagging gate that led into a sandy front yard scattered with ice plant and thistles. Val disguised her dismay. It was more dilapidated and forlorn than she had imagined. Nonetheless, they were here.

She was fighting exhaustion as she paid the driver, then thanked him for carrying two of her suitcases up to the porch while she staggered in her high heels with the other two bags and the groceries. With a sinking heart, she watched him drive back down the rutted road and disappear. Suddenly, she felt alone and abandoned.

Megan, however, was delighted with everything. She squatted down and sifted the sand through both chubby hands. "Look, Mommy, it's just like my sandbox at home only lots bigger."

Thank God for Megan, Val said, meaning it like a prayer. Without her, she would have given in to despair.

Inside, Val did a quick walk-through of the practically bare rooms. Whatever it was, it's home for now, Val told herself firmly. She would make the best of it. She was determined.

She had gone on enough camping trips with her parents to be fairly adept at getting the small two-burner gas stove lighted to heat a can of tomato soup. That done, she got a fire going in the potbellied stove. It gave out an amazing amount of heat once it caught. Again, it was Megan's cheerful presence that kept Val from giving way to the hovering fear that seemed to lurk in the shadowy corners of the empty rooms.

She made up the beds and gradually Megan wound down. Yawning sleepily, she climbed into the little cot in the bedroom. Val had tucked her in when all at once Megan's eyes popped wide open and she said, "Prayers, Mommy."

Val was stricken. She'd completely forgotten. A little child shall lead them, Val thought guiltily. Hastily, she came back and knelt beside Megan.

Clasping her small hands together and closing her eyes, Megan began, "Thank you God for our nice little house and the beach just over the dunes. Bless Mommy and Harriet and Flynn." Megan halted, a little pucker in her forehead. "You think Flynn misses us, Mommy?"

"I'm sure he does, darling, but Harriet promised she and Lew would take good care of him, so don't worry."

"Can we have him soon since we've got a new place? There's lots of room for him to run here, don't you think?"

"We'll see, darling." Val gave the answer she used to hate to hear from her own parents. But there was no help for it. She couldn't make a promise to Megan she couldn't keep.

Megan squeezed her eyes tight, and folding her hands again, she added, "And God bless Daddy, too." Those words were like a sharp knife in Val's heart. How much did Megan know? What had she gleaned from everything that had been going on around her all these weeks, hushed conversations, telephone calls, the changes, the appearance of strangers, the absence of friends?

God bless Daddy. The child's innocent prayer echoed in Val's mind. Oh, Kevin! Why did you let this happen?

Val leaned down and kissed Megan, holding her in a tight hug for a minute. It took an effort not to let the tears that pressed the back of her eyes fall. "Good night, precious," she whispered as she kissed her again before she left the room. A minute later, she looked in and Megan was sound asleep.

It was then the awful loneliness descended. Val shivered as if from a freezing wind. She huddled by the stove far into the night. Finally, it sputtered out, and not wanting to use more of the logs than necessary, she crept into bed. But she couldn't get warm. The cold seemed to penetrate into her bones. She buried her face into the pillow, smothering her sobs, not wanting to wake Megan. Her misery was deep and terrible. Even so, Val realized whatever she was going through could not compare with what Kevin must be enduring. *Oh, God, help him, please,* she moaned a quiet prayer. A man like Kevin could go mad, locked up in a cell like an animal in a cage. *Have mercy, Lord.*

Chapter Four

Val got up carefully so as not to awaken Megan. It was early, but that wasn't unusual for her now. She hadn't slept well at all during these past few months. After tossing and turning half the night, her sleep distorted by dreams, she would wake up before dawn. She'd told herself that it was her worry about Kevin that kept her awake. Once the initial shock was over, she'd hoped her insomnia would get better.

But now there were new anxieties. She would be on the brink of sleep when suddenly the fact that she and Megan were completely alone in the world would bring her to instant wakefulness. She would lie there trembling, realizing they were without family or friends, miles from everyone and everything familiar. No backup. No support, emotional or financial, available if anything happened. An emergency of some sort. Frightening possibilities flashed through her imagination. What if she got sick or had some kind of breakdown, what would happen to Megan? Val would look over at the little girl sleeping so peacefully and a fierce determination would follow. She refused to give in to that fear. She reminded herself that at least now they had a place to live and she had a promise of a job. She had to be strong for Megan's sake. They would make it, please God.

Shivering in the damp chill of the unheated cottage, Val put on her robe and hurried out to the front room to get the stove going. After nearly a week's practice, she had become better at getting a fire started. The small stove provided a good amount of heat for the place and she could also cook on it if she didn't want to use the gas stove. It was amazing what you could get used to, Val thought as she filled the kettle with water to boil so she could make coffee. How much she had taken for granted before in her home in Meadowbrook. A flick of a switch and within minutes the house would be comfortably warm. An automatic coffeemaker set the night before would have fresh coffee waiting when she came into the kitchen.

Val didn't allow much mental wandering back to the old life, but sometimes comparisons were inevitable. But every day she gained a little confidence that things were going to work out. Each step she took on her own gave her the courage to take the next one. She was doing her best to accomplish what Kevin had asked—to build a new life for herself and Megan. She measured instant coffee into a mug, poured in the boiling water, stirred it until the crystals dissolved, then took it over to the window and looked out.

It was beginning to get light. The wind off the ocean was chopping the gray-blue sea into haphazard waves. Seagulls in search of breakfast were gliding and dipping in a kind of frenzied ballet. Glancing to her left, down the stretch of winter beach, she saw smoke coming from one of the other cottages. It was the last one in the staggered line of weathered shingled houses.

Vaguely, she wondered who else had come to this isolated place at this time of year. It didn't really matter. Val knew that she couldn't risk friendships. One thing led to another on the slightest acquaintance. People expected a certain amount of information about your background, where you'd come from, what you were doing. Although Val had always liked getting to know people, that was something her present circumstances didn't allow anymore.

Again came the clang of her own prison door. It might be invisible, but it was nonetheless real. Her promise to Kev had shut out the possibility of her having any normal contact with other people, no matter how casual. She would have to guard against the temptation, simply out of loneliness, of getting friendly with anyone. It would be so easy to let something slip. And she had to protect Megan at all costs. That's what Kevin had wanted. Correction, *insisted* on her doing.

Val remembered how she used to worry that Kev didn't spend enough time with Megan, play with her enough, pay enough attention to her. Afraid, that, maybe he didn't even love her enough. Especially after the problem with her hearing was discovered. Yet it was his concern for Megan that had prompted his adamant insistence on Val taking her someplace where no one would know about him. Surely, that must prove how much he did love her.

Val turned back from the window and looked around the room. The shabbiness of the place was even more depressing in daytime. There were the usual beach-rental castoffs: a wicker set consisting of a love seat and two armchairs, a table, a couple of straight chairs, a lopsided bookcase. It needed brightening badly. It wouldn't take a whole lot or cost much to do. Val had always been sensitive to her surroundings. She decided that living in this drab, barren cottage would drive her crazy if she didn't do something about it.

Just then, Megan woke up and called from the bedroom, "Mommy, what can we do today? Can we go to the beach?" Val smiled. Megan wanted to go to the beach every day since they had come to the cottage. She came running out in her nightie. "Please, Mommy, can we?" she begged, hopping from one foot to the other.

Val grabbed her up in a hug, swung her around. "It's still pretty cold, honey. But we're going to have a fun day. Today we're going to go shopping and get some pretty curtains and maybe new bedspreads and some pillows. You can pick out the kind you like, okay?"

Megan had never before been consulted on decorating and the idea was a new and exciting prospect.

Very much aware of her dwindling funds, Val felt this was not an extravagance but a necessary expense. An investment in her well-being. She had noticed a variety store between the Realtor's and the post office so that's where they headed. It was only a short walk to the center of Seawood and Megan was a merry little companion.

They found some café curtains patterned with sunflowers and several toss pillows in bright patterns. Megan chose pink chenille bedspreads. To her relief, Val found their combined purchases totaled little more than fifty dollars. She was satisfied that whatever the cost it was well worth it. How little it took to make a child happy, she thought, watching Megan skip happily ahead of her down the street.

On the way home, they stopped for fish and chips at a small fish market and ate at a picnic table outside in view of the ocean. A pale sun had come out and the sea was a deep royal blue with bobbing whitecaps.

"I love it here, Mommy," Megan said suddenly. "Can we stay here forever?"

Val's heart contracted. Forever? Forever is a long time. How do you measure forever? For her, even five years, the soonest Kevin could come up for parole, seemed forever. Even the weeks since his arrest seemed forever. But she managed to answer Megan's question. "Well, darling, we'll certainly be living here for a while."

Brightening up the little cottage helped a lot. So did a change in the weather. The morning fog seemed to burn off earlier and they began to have longer sunny afternoons, which more and more they spent at the beach. Megan never tired of digging in the sand, hunting for shells or poking at sand crabs. They took long walks along the edge of the water, playing tag with the tide, picking up driftwood. Where the beach rounded a rocky bend, they discovered a sheltered cove that they claimed as their own special place.

Sometimes, when watching Megan running back and forth from the ocean back to the sand, her golden hair flying behind her in the wind, or hunched over a tide pool, earnestly studying the tiny sea creatures, Val would feel a wrench. How sad that Kevin was missing so much of Megan's evolving little person. She knew that was futile thinking, even harmful. She had to go on. Live in the present, not dwell in the past, nor in pointless regrets. Take one day at a time.

One thing she could not push aside, or think about without concern, was Kevin's total lack of communication. She had done everything he asked except for the divorce. She felt he had made that decision under extreme duress. Val was convinced it was a wrong decision. It was the act of a man desperate and despairing. Hadn't they promised each other "for better or for worse"? Well, this was the worst either of them could ever have imagined. She prayed he would change his mind when he had time to consider it. He would want her to wait for him.

Val had read that men in prison need one thing more than anything else. Hope. Hope that someone would be waiting when they'd done their time. That they would have something, someone, to come back to, to help them make a fresh start, turn over a new leaf. Val wanted to give Kevin that.

So she had written him several letters. So far he hadn't answered. But she wasn't willing to give up. He had to have a period of adjustment to prison life. Then maybe he'd allow himself to think of her and Megan, to miss them, to long for some connection. That's what she was praying for, was trusting would happen. If the loneliness she was experiencing was sometimes more than she could bear, what must it be for Kevin? Kevin, the energetic, outgoing person she knew, one who loved having company in, going out. The confinement of prison, the enforced company of hardened criminals—it must be terrible for him.

But he didn't write. Day after day, Val watched the blue-and-white snub-nosed mail truck go by, never stopping at their mailbox. They never got any mail. Except some circulars marked Occupant. That shouldn't seem strange. No one knew where they were even if there had been somebody to write. Val decided not to request a box at the post office. She would have had to fill out an application supplying all sorts of information. She'd also heard that small-town post offices were the center for local gossip. Val didn't dare have people in Seawood speculating about her.

She wondered if Kevin had any idea what lengths she was having to go to keep her word to him? More and more Val realized she had been sentenced along with Kevin to her own kind of prison.

Chapter Five

Val assured herself that things would get better once she started work. Once they had some regular routine to their life and a weekly paycheck. And they did.

For one thing, she was too tired at night to lie awake and worry. The job at the restaurant gave a structure to her days. The McDermotts were great employers. There had been a preseason orientation week for the new staff. The other waitresses were friendly and pleasant. Most of them had had more waitressing experience than Val, but she found them ready to help her learn the ropes.

Best of all, Val found a good sitter for Megan through Colleen, one of the other waitresses. Her sister was a young mom with two small youngsters. She was eager to earn the extra money and Megan needed the companionship of other children. Val dropped Megan off at Sue's house on her way to work and picked her up on the way home. Things were working out much better than Val could have hoped. Except for one important thing.

There still was no word from Kevin. He had not answered any of Val's letters. Every week she wrote another one, begging him to let her come see him. But day after day she checked the mail and there was nothing. It had been two months now since that awful day in the courtroom. Surely the loneliness must be getting to Kevin. Maybe her letters had been too reassuring, maybe he thought they were doing okay, that he had done the right thing and was determined not to make contact. Val turned all the possibilities over and over in her mind. Nothing made sense. How could Kevin just eliminate them like pressing Delete on a computer?

Finally, Val wrote to the prison asking for information on visiting schedules. She then wrote a second letter and addressed it to the warden's office, explaining that she had heard nothing from her husband and asking for a progress report.

After she mailed it, Val felt frightened and guilty. Kevin had been almost violent that day when he insisted she was to forget him.

Since high school, Kevin had been the most important person in Val's life. She had loved Kevin almost from the first. He was a street-smart kid from the wrong side of the tracks in their small conservative California hometown. His boldness attracted her, while at the same time, she also saw a vulnerable, insecure side of him that drew her sympathy and love.

Her schoolteacher parents had strongly objected to and tried to discourage their relationship. But their opposition only fueled the fire of their romance. They had continued to see each other secretly and the summer after Val graduated high school they eloped. Val's parents' attempt to have the marriage annulled was abandoned, but the estrangement from their daughter and her husband lasted until their deaths a few years ago.

Two years ahead of Val in high school, Kevin had excelled in sports. He'd been a track star and won an athletic scholarship to college. Upon graduation, he'd been recruited into the executive-training program of one of the large Bay area chain of banks. He had made rapid progress, moving up with successive promotions to the position of a loan officer at one of the branches. In that position, Kevin was able to indulge his expensive tastes. His personality, always brash, by thirty-two had become supremely self-confident. Although some people thought him arrogant, Val made excuses for him because she understood that his behavior masked left-over insecurities from childhood. However, it was the reckless side of him, the side that liked taking chances, gambling, that in the end brought him down. Success had come too soon, too easily.

After sending off the letter to the warden, Val lived on hope. Three weeks dragged by and there was no reply. Then one day she found a letter in her mailbox. It had a return address she did not recognize. It wasn't from the prison. Curious, she tore open the envelope, drew out the typed, single-spaced letter. The signature identified the writer as Chaplain Scott, the prison chaplain. Her letter had been referred to him by the warden.

Your husband is having an unusually difficult time adjusting to prison life. For some men the adjustment is more severe than for others. This may be the case with your husband. It sometimes takes six months or more for a man to finally accept the fact of being in prison and decide he has to make the best of his term of imprisonment.

The only advice I can give you is to be patient. I have tried to talk to him, but he refuses to discuss with me his reasons for not writing to you. When your husband has completed the required probationary period before he can receive visitors, you will be notified.

In the meantime, perhaps if you continue to write the kind of loving, supportive letters you indicated you have been writing to him, in due time he may reply.

If I can be of any further assistance to you, please feel free to write to me.

Val replaced the letter in the envelope. She felt let down, discouraged. In spite of the chaplain's suggestion, it seemed pointless to continue trying. Was Kevin even reading her letters? Would he continue to hold out? For all her disappointment, deep down inside Val a spark burned, a small, persistent flame of hope.

Once, Kevin had loved her. Their physical passion had been real. He had always had the "you and me against the world" attitude. That couldn't have changed. He couldn't have forgotten all that they'd been through together. They had weathered other storms, hurdled obstacles even to be with each other, to marry. This was the biggest challenge—the biggest tragedy—they'd ever faced. The words "seven to fifteen years" rang in Val's memory. Could their marriage somehow survive this? She shuddered.

Val put the letter in her dresser drawer. Every once in a while during the weeks that followed, she'd take it out and read it. The possibility of change, the hope the chaplain had held out, was like a life raft. She clung to it the way a drowning person clutches at a straw. After all, it was all she had.

Chapter Six

After Memorial Day weekend, the restaurant was busy, but the work was not all that hard. Seawood was actually off the beaten track. Most people coming south from San Francisco were on their way to Carmel, the ones going north heading up into redwood country. Only the most leisurely of travelers, not in a hurry to get anywhere particular, took the off-ramp from the freeway and discovered The Seawind.

Val's hours gave her lots of quality time with Megan. As they went into summer, the long, lovely days were perfect beach weather. She'd pack a basket of snacks, a thermos of lemonade, then the two of them would walk down to the little inlet they'd begun to call their "secret cove." There they would spread out a blanket and Megan would play happily in the sand, building roads, tunnels and castles, running into the shallow water, then carrying back her small bucket of water. Sometimes, Val brought a magazine or a paperback to read, but mostly she would watch Megan.

Children are marvelous, she thought. How quickly they adjust to new circumstances. Megan seemed con-

tent and secure. All Val had told her was that Kevin had
to be away for a while. That seemed to satisfy her. She
didn't seem to miss him and rarely mentioned her father
except in her nighttime prayers. To Val, that seemed a
shame, but that's the way Kevin had wanted it. Megan's
precious days of early childhood were something that
could never be replaced. Even as Val watched her, she
was changing from day to day. This time was slipping
away just as Megan's sand castles were washed away
in the surf. And Kevin was missing them.

By summer, the other three cottages were sometimes
rented for weekends. One family came for a week. Most
of the time they were empty. Better accommodations
for vacationers could be found in other places nearby.
But as far as Val could tell, the cottage at the far end,
the one she'd seen smoke coming from, remained un-
occupied. She never explored that part of the beach. It
would have meant passing by the other cottages, perhaps running into one of the renters. She still avoided
even the briefest conversation with anyone other than
the people at work.

As the weeks went by, Val began to lose hope that
Kevin would write. She continued her weekly letter
to him although she was finding it harder to fill more
than a page. There was less and less to say. There was
no more heartbroken pleading, no declarations that she
disagreed with his decision. Little by little her spark of
faith began to flicker and go out.

On the surface, their life seemed as smooth as the
sea on a windless day. No one would ever have guessed
the emotional turmoil that was always just under the
surface. Megan was happy and as friendly as a little

puppy. She soon became the restaurant's pet. The other waitresses called her their mascot while the chef was always sending treats home for her, little lemon tarts or iced petits fours. The McDermotts doted on her almost as if she were one of their grandchildren. Tom always wanted Val to bring her by before she took her to the sitter's. Both McDermotts were so kind Val began to feel guilty she hadn't told them the truth about Kevin. What would they say if they knew she was living a lie?

The atmosphere at The Seawinds was so friendly, the food so delicious and the staff trained to treat customers like visiting royalty that the tips were more than generous. Val was able to stash away a nice nest egg that she hoped would tide her over the months when the restaurant was closed for the season. She hoped she could find some other temporary job; even a part-time position would help. She wasn't looking that far ahead yet, but she knew Seawinds would close in November. The McDermotts went to Mexico for several months until the restaurant reopened in the spring.

Because she was busy with work and had gradually given up any hope of hearing from Kevin, Val was totally unprepared for what happened toward the end of August. Another letter came from the prison chaplain. Almost afraid to open it, Val finally read it with mixed feelings. The chaplain said Kevin seemed to be making some progress toward adjustment but that he continued to find him uncommunicative and still refusing to discuss anything personal. Kevin had passed the six-month probationary period and was now allowed to have visitors. However, he advised Val not to come unless Kevin himself wrote and requested it.

Val read the letter through twice, then once again more slowly, letting the impact of each word sift through the jumbled thoughts crowding into her head. If she waited until Kevin wrote and asked—that might be never! She knew how stubborn Kevin could be. Even if he wanted her, Val felt sure he would not write and ask.

The letter had come just before Val left for work. She put it in her apron pocket where it lay like a burning coal all during her shift. Later, when she got home, she read the letter again. Finally, she decided she had to go see him. Maybe when he saw her he would realize what a mistake it was to cut himself off like this and insist that they divorce.

But how was she to get some time off to travel the considerable distance to the state prison? And how would she explain it to the McDermotts? Val knew she could trade hours with one or two of the other waitresses, but it was the peak of the season. The Seawinds was always filled with hungry customers. It would be like that until after Labor Day, some of the staff warned. If she was going, she would need at least two full days off. How could she ask without telling Mrs. McDermott the reason?

It was Kevin's day in court all over again. Val tried to control her nervousness as she lingered at the end of the shift, waiting for an opportunity to speak to Eileen McDermott. The dinner crowd had gone, the busboys were bundling up tablecloths, stacking up plates, and there was a clatter of trays and murmur of voices as they talked and joked with each other. Mrs. McDermott was behind the cash register. Val watched for the right moment to approach her.

"May I talk to you privately for a few minutes?" she asked in a low voice.

"Sure, Val, what can I do for you?" Mrs. McDermott smiled.

Val couldn't help wondering how long the smile would last when she knew that Val's reason for wanting time off was to visit her husband in prison. She glanced uneasily around, then whispered, "Do you think we could go into your office. I don't want to be overheard."

Mrs. McDermott looked puzzled, but she agreed at once. "Of course." She led the way into her small, cozy office behind the dining room. She sat down on one of the two chintz-covered armchairs and gestured to Val to take the other one. "Now, Val, what's on your mind? You look mighty serious. I hope you're not going to tell me you're quitting?" She gave Val a wary look.

"No, not at all, Mrs. McDermott. I love it here, I like my job. It's just—I need some time off, but first, there's something I should have told you in the beginning."

Telling the facts turned out to be a great deal easier than Val had anticipated. Eileen McDermott listened with a thoughtful expression. Val's voice rose and fell and became breathless as she poured out the whole awful story. Tears came perilously close and she struggled to hold them back. When she finished, she saw only sympathy and concern in the older woman's eyes. Instead of being shocked or judgmental, she just gently scolded Val for thinking she wouldn't understand.

"Of course you can take the time off, Val, and I think you should go."

Val couldn't bring herself to tell her that Kevin didn't want to see her, that he might even refuse to see her once she got there. She was too relieved that her employer had been so understanding and there would be no problem about taking time off. Not only that, but Mrs. McDermott insisted Val leave Megan with them and save baby-sitting fees.

"You know Tom will be tickled to death to have her. Now, it's settled. You go ahead and make your plans."

The night before Val was to leave, she nearly lost her nerve. It had been six months since that dreadful day in the bare little room in the courthouse when Kevin had brutally shaken off her embrace, violently demanded she get a divorce. She had no idea how he would react when she showed up at the prison. Well, ready or not, it was a chance she'd have to take. In her heart, she felt it was the right thing to do. Give them both another chance.

Val studied herself in the mirror. Kevin would find her changed. She had lost at least five pounds, which, on her small frame, made her look almost thin. She had stopped highlighting her hair, letting it return to its natural brown color. Not able to afford the expensive styling she used to get, she had cut it herself. Very short. With almost daily dips in the ocean before she went to work, this length was much easier. But would Kev like it?

What should she wear for this visit? She hadn't worn anything but her uniform, and jeans or shorts or a bathing suit for months. Kev had always been highly critical of her appearance, telling her what he liked and what he didn't like in no uncertain terms. She wanted to look her best no matter what. It would be especially important when he saw her for the first time in all these months.

After trying on first one thing and then the next, she finally decided on a blue, washed-silk shirtwaist dress. It was Kev's favorite color and wouldn't wrinkle badly in her small suitcase.

Val stopped fussing over her own appearance long enough to get Megan packed up and the next morning, she took her to the McDermotts. Megan was thrilled with the novelty of staying over with the McDermotts. After Val kissed her goodbye, she went happily hand in hand with Tom down to his boat.

"Don't worry, she'll be fine," Eileen assured her and wished her a good trip. Val thanked her again, then hurried off to where the northbound bus stopped.

Chapter Seven

On the long bus trip, Val had a lot of time to think about what she would say to Kevin. She didn't even know if he had read her letters or just torn them up. Maybe it didn't matter. Maybe she should have written to the chaplain, telling him she had decided to come, then he could have prepared Kev for her visit. Maybe she should phone his office at one of the rest stops? Maybe, maybe, so many things. But maybe none of it mattered? She was on her way now. There was no turning back.

Her stomach was in knots most of the way. The hours of travel seemed endless, the bus crowded and the trip a jolting one, up twisting mountain roads, long stretches of highway bordered with brooding wooded hills as they got closer to the isolated site of the state prison.

At last, early in the evening, they reached the town above which the penitentiary was located. It was dreary beyond description. Fog swirled eerily as Val made her way down the dingy main street to a small hotel the bus driver told her was about the only decent place in town to stay. She thought he had looked at her with something like sympathy mixed with curiosity. When she asked him directions, she felt her face grow warm. Did he know why she was here in this town at this time of night? And what difference did that make? It was just her own sense of shame. He probably brought busloads of relatives of prison inmates here all the time. It was nothing new to him. Her private agony meant nothing to him.

Worn out from the long bus ride and nerves, Val fell into an exhausted sleep. She woke up long before it was time to catch the local bus up to the prison. Val knew about that from the brochure on visiting procedures she'd received when she wrote for information. As she dressed, her heart was beating so fast she could hardly breathe. She brushed her hair, put on lipstick with a shaky hand. In the bathroom mirror, under the glaring light over the sink, she looked deathly pale. She dusted on blusher. Okay? She kept trying to see herself through Kevin's eyes. Then she shivered. That was the best she could do.

Outside, she walked across the street to the bus station and bought coffee at the snack counter. It was weak and tasted terrible in the paper cup, so she only took a few sips. Was it time yet? She glanced down at the dainty diamond-chip wristwatch Kevin had given her when he got his first promotion at the bank. It was too ornate to wear at work, but Val had worn it today thinking Kevin might like to see it on her.

She looked around at the other people in the station. There were several women of various ages. A few sat together, talking in low voices. A few sat apart, faces set in misery. Were they all going up to the prison, too?

Most were poorly dressed, worn-looking. Val turned away. She shouldn't be staring. She was embarrassed for them. A core of bitterness she rarely admitted stirred inside her. Resentment that Kevin had put her in this position. Humiliation seared her. Why should she feel superior to these women? She was in exactly the same situation they were.

The door to the loading platform opened and a driver announced, "Bus now boarding." There was a general movement as the passengers in the waiting room, mostly women, gathered up bundles and packages, then started toward the door. For a minute, Val hesitated. She didn't want to file out there with the others, admit she was going to the prison to visit an inmate. Then quickly she felt ashamed. Whatever she was feeling, what Kevin must be feeling all these months was worse. She straightened her shoulders and walked out to the bus.

From the bus window, the outline of the huge gray prison loomed ahead like a medieval fortress as the bus wound its way up the narrow road. The facility had been built on a cliff overlooking the ocean to provide maximum security for prisoners who might think of escaping. When it had been built, the word was put out, and since then the legend had grown that no one ever escaped from this penal institution. That bleak view was what Kevin had to look out at every day. That is, if there was a window in his cell.

The bus stopped at the prison gates, and everyone filed down the aisles and out. Val realized she had been right; all the passengers were on the same mission. Visitors. She wondered if the wives of prisoners had some kind of distinguishing mark? Something that identified them as indelibly as the numbers stamped on inmates' clothes. Or maybe they were only recognizable to a fellow sufferer.

Even though the day was warming, Val kept shivering, had to press her lips together to keep her teeth from chattering.

At a wire-windowed enclosure at the gate, they had to present identification to a uniformed guard. From there go through a metal detector before passing through the gates into an inner courtyard. Here they went single file through a door marked Visitors into a large empty room with wooden benches along one side. A half-glass partition divided the room. On the visitors' side were shelves, a telephone and a straight chair. The guard indicated they were to sit down until the name lists were checked, inmates who were to receive visitors notified.

They waited for what seemed at least half an hour. No one spoke. Even the women who had been murmuring together at the bus station were now wrapped in a tense silence. No one more than Val. She glanced around. Probably most of these other women were expected. Their husbands, boyfriends, brothers were looking forward to seeing them. Her case was different. Her hands clenched compulsively. Suddenly, an electric bell shrilled, causing her to jump. Through the glass, she saw a door on the other side open and a line of men in drab prison garb filed into the room.

Val held her breath, searching for a glimpse of Kevin among them. Then saw him and suppressed a cry. She half rose, waving her hand. The guard barked out the names and motioned the women forward as prisoners moved into places on the other side.

Kev was scowling. Val was sure he had not been able to figure out who his visitor was. Maybe he thought it might be Brad Hensley, his lawyer. When he saw her, his eyes widened, he flushed a deep red, then his mouth settled into a straight line. But he walked to the seat as she hurried to the window opposite.

Nothing could have prepared Val for what prison life had done to her husband. It was the physical changes in his appearance that were the most shocking. He looked much older. His eyes were dull, the eyelids puffy. The tan he cultivated so diligently had faded, replaced by a grayness that almost matched the rough denim shirt. Kev had always been a "fitness freak," maintaining his body with rigid discipline. Now there was a slackness about him; he looked soft, pudgy. He slumped into the chair. Somewhere, Val had read modern prisons had exercise rooms where prisoners could work out, pump iron, keep in shape. Was this another of the options offered to inmates that Kevin had refused to take advantage of?

Val tried to conceal her dismay at the way he'd deteriorated. She took her place opposite him, picked up the phone and said huskily, "Hi, darling." Kevin did not pick up the receiver on his side. Instead, he folded his arms across his chest, his expression like stone. He avoided making eye contact. Val tried again. "Please, Kev. We must talk."

Reluctantly, he lifted the phone. Between clenched teeth, he said, "I told you not to come."

"I know, Kev. But I had to come. Darling, don't you

see what you're doing is wrong? Wrong for Megan, wrong for me, wrong for you. Please, try to understand, I can't let you blot us out of your life like this."

"I thought I made it clear I didn't want you to come. You should have done what I told you," he said harshly. "It was stupid of you to think I'd change my mind." His expression hardened. "Brad—my lawyer—" he almost spit out the word, so Val guessed he must have met with some recent coldness from his onetime friend "—tells me you haven't returned the divorce papers. I want you to sign them."

"I can't sign them. I don't want to end our marriage. Listen, Kevin, it's going to be all right, I promise you. I did what you asked. I moved out of town to Seawood. Remember Seawood? Anyway, I'm using my maiden name so Megan is protected and I've got a job and a place to live. We're doing okay. Of course, we miss you terribly, and when you're free—"

"I'll never be free of the stink of prison. It will cling to me for the rest of my life. Don't you realize it's over for us? For you and me? Things will never be the same. Don't you get it? Or are you too stupid?" he shouted. Val saw the man on the other side of Kevin glance at him. The guard walking back and forth along the line of prisoners halted, watching him.

Val winced. She knew that when Kevin was angry or upset he said things, terrible things sometimes, things he didn't mean, things he was sorry for afterward. Half the presents he gave her were offered in apology for some tirade or other. She'd learned to expect both. The explosion, then the remorse.

If she just remained composed, kept Kevin talking,

maybe she could calm him down, make him see how important her coming was for all of them, their future. But she didn't have a chance. Kevin leaned forward, his face very close to the glass partition, the phone next to his mouth.

"Now listen, Val, I want you to do exactly what I say. Don't delay any longer on the divorce. I don't want you to come here again. Ever, understand? You're young and smart and you'll make it. I want you to be free. You'll meet someone and get married again—"

"No, no, you're wrong, Kev. I won't. I don't want to. I—"

"Shut up!" Kev yelled. Stunned, Val drew back, almost dropping the phone. Kev's voice was so loud everyone could hear it in spite of the partition. "Didn't I tell you not to come here? Don't you ever come back or try to see me again. You hear me? And you sign those papers, you hear?"

With that, Kevin slammed down the phone, then stood, pushing back and knocking over the chair. It crashed onto the concrete floor. Without a backward glance, Kevin flung himself away and stalked to the door leading back to the main part of the prison.

Chapter Eight

The buzz of other voices, magnified in the high-ceilinged room, halted abruptly, everyone shocked into silence by Kevin's outburst. Val sat there, paralyzed. She felt the blood rush into her face. Kev's fury had lashed like a stinging whip. Dazed, she somehow managed to get to her feet, then stood for a minute, dizzy with humiliation. Mercifully, the other visitors looked away, resuming their own conversations while she headed blindly toward the exit.

The outer door was opened by the guard and Val brushed by not knowing whether he looked at her with contempt or compassion. She hurried down the long corridor and was given clearance to leave from the security guard at the next door. She walked stiffly to the gate where another guard drew back the bolt and at last she stumbled outside into the glare of hazy sunlight. She let out a long breath not realizing she had been holding it. She stood uncertainly, not knowing where to go, what to do. She wasn't sure when there would be another bus back to the small town. She'd just have to walk down to the bus shelter and wait. One was bound to come along in a while.

She was too numb to cry. She felt bruised by the brutality of Kevin's reaction. His rejection had been total. Wobbling a little on her high heels, Val went down the steep hill. It was almost funny. She had only worn these pumps because Kev had always liked to see her in high heels. A pale sun struggled through the overcast. It was turning into a pretty day.

As Val made her way to the bus shelter, her mind was trying to make sense of it all. It seemed incredible that out here the sun was shining, flowers blooming along the roadside, birds singing, people driving by in cars and RVs, going on vacation. How could life continue so normally when hers had fallen apart? Her heart twisted in pity for Kev and all the men who, for whatever reason, were locked inside the prison where the sun never entered, where life was grim, gray, hopeless.

When she reached the bus stop, she saw that another woman was already seated there. She looked like she might have been shedding a few tears but glanced the other way as Val took a seat at the other end of the wooden bench.

Everything about the visit had gone wrong, Val thought. She'd meant it to be so different, even rehearsed being cheerful and positive. And it had all ended so badly. The tears she hadn't shed now began to rush into her eyes. She'd even forgotten to show Kev Megan's crayon drawings. She hadn't had a chance.

She opened her handbag and fumbled for a tissue. She pulled out her compact, powdered her nose and freshened her lipstick. In the mirror, she saw the other woman looking at her. Val put her things back in her purse, then looked back at her. Their glances met and they measured each other slowly. Then, as if instinctively acknowledging they were in the same boat, the woman nodded and smiled faintly. A few minutes later, she got up and moved over to sit beside Val. She jerked her head in the direction of the prison.

"You been up there to see your man, too?"

"Yes," Val answered.

"Awful, isn't it? For weeks you look forward to coming and when you're face-to-face you wish you hadn't come. Sometimes Jack's okay, but other times…" Her voice trailed away and she shook her head. "It's all so unnatural. If we could just hold hands, if he could touch me." She sighed heavily. "I love my husband. A lot. But I don't know if a marriage can last with this kind of physical separation."

Val tensed. What this woman was saying came from her heart, from a depth of experience that she herself was just entering.

"I'm sure he wonders the same thing. And I know his biggest fear is getting out and not having anyone to come home to. I know from the way he acts sometimes when I visit that it's been getting to him. Every so often he breaks down when I'm there, tells me that night after night he lies in his bunk wondering where I am, what I'm doing, and if I'm being faithful. It's torture."

She took out a pack of cigarettes, offered it to Val, who shook her head. Then she reached inside her handbag for a small lighter, flicked it and lit her cigarette.

"Jack's in on his second offense, this time car theft. Would you believe he smashed up the car before they arrested him? Now he's seeing the prison psychiatrist to see what makes him do it." She inhaled deeply and blew the smoke out with a bitter laugh. "Maybe I'm the one who should see a shrink. I must be nuts to love a guy like him."

She smoked silently for a few minutes and Val studied her. She was probably Val's age or even younger, pretty in a kind of flashy way. Her hair was blond, with help, and she wore a great deal of makeup. Maybe that was the way Jack liked her to look and dress. Maybe she was just like me, Val thought sadly, trying to please her man. Maybe that's why we ended up with the kind of men we had.

"Jack's forty now, he'll be nearly fifty by the time he gets out. He's not learning any skills in prison. I don't have a clue as to what he'll do when he does get out. An ex-con has a hard enough time getting any kind of job. But an ex-con who's almost fifty with no skills, well, the outlook for a guy like that is probably zilch."

Her words struck Val with their harsh truth. Kevin would also be an ex-con when he got out. He must know that, too. That might be adding to his bitterness, his depression. Kev had always gotten by on his looks, his charm, his self-assured can-do attitude. Prison had been the ultimate defeat.

The woman was speaking again, almost as if to herself.

"I don't know if I can stick it out. When I think of eight more years. Making this trip once a month to see him for an hour or less. Especially after a bad one like we had today. I don't know whether it's worth it." She shook her head vigorously, causing her red plastic hoop earrings to swing. "Yeah, sometimes I really wonder. The loneliness, the hopelessness... I don't think those guys, the judges who do the sentencing, realize they're sentencing the wives and families of those men to the same amount of time. And I begin to think, wouldn't it be better to cut your losses and try to make a new start while you're still young enough...?"

Her voice trailed off because just then the bus came into view and they boarded. There weren't two seats together so they each found a separate seat. In a way, Val was glad. The other woman's words had echoed hollowly in her heart. They mirrored her own half-formed conclusions about her own situation.

However, when they got to the bus station in town, the other woman was standing on the platform waiting for her. "You wouldn't want to go somewhere and talk some more, I guess?" she asked doubtfully.

Val didn't want to seem unfriendly, but she knew it wouldn't be a good idea. She was already depressed enough. What purpose would it serve for either of them? They had the same problem and they each would have to handle it the best way they could.

"I'm sorry, but I can't," Val said gently. "Someone is taking care of my little girl for me and I think I better take the next bus home. Thanks anyway."

The woman nodded as if she understood, then shrugged. "Well, so long and good luck," she said, and walked away down the street where a neon sign blinked Cocktails.

Back in the bus station, Val realized her head was pounding. She remembered she hadn't eaten all day. She couldn't have eaten anything. Even now her stomach was in knots from her emotional stress. She bought a small box of aspirin and got a soda from the soft-drink dispenser to wash two of them down. Hopefully, she could sleep on the bus back to Seawood. She didn't want to think or even feel. Oblivion sounded like a wonderful escape after all she'd been through.

Chapter Nine

By the time the bus pulled into Seawood, Val was bone tired. She had not been able to sleep on the bus as she had hoped. She felt wired. Over and over she replayed the scene with Kevin, his words repeating themselves again and again in her brain. If this was what he really wanted, then what? She wondered how he could still love her or Megan at all and be able to insist that they break all ties so coldly, so irrevocably. What did she do with the rest of her life? Hers and Megan's? Of course, there was no immediate answer.

Shaky, sick, almost feverish, Val was shivering when she got off the bus. She called Eileen McDermott from a pay phone and asked if it would be all right for Megan to stay over until the next day. Mrs. McDermott assured Val that it would be fine.

"As a matter of fact, she's already in her pajamas and watching TV with Tom. I was just about to serve them both ice cream when you called." There was a slight pause, then she asked, "How did it go?"

"Not great," Val answered. From Val's tone of voice,

Eileen must have guessed how weary she was and didn't ask any more questions.

"You get a good night's sleep," she just said, "and we'll see you tomorrow. Don't worry, Megan is as happy as a little clam."

"Thanks, I can't tell you how much I appreciate—"

"Don't try." Eileen cut her off. "It's been our pleasure. Megan is a doll."

Val let herself into the dark, empty cottage and closed the door behind her. Alone, she didn't have to put on a good front or be brave for anyone. It was then the whole horrible experience kicked in and she began to shake uncontrollably. In spite of the warm evening, she felt cold. Moving like a robot, she went over to the stove, crumpled up some newspaper, threw on a few wood chips and stood there, her arms wrapped around her upper body, until the fire caught hold. She pulled up one of the chairs in front of the stove, hunching there trying to get warm and to figure out what she was going to do, how to put the pieces of her shattered hopes into some endurable whole.

Over and over in her mind, Val went through all that she had wanted to say to Kevin. To tell him that she'd done most of what he had wanted her to do except for the divorce. She'd moved to this remote little spot, changed her name, given no one, not even Harriet, a forwarding address. There was no way anyone connected with the bank or our old neighborhood could trace them here. She was an ordinary single mom, working as a waitress, raising a little girl by herself, doing the best she could. Nobody except Mrs. McDermott knew she was the wife of a convicted embezzler. No reason why after Kevin served his time, they couldn't move somewhere else, start their life together again as a family. It didn't make sense to break up their marriage.

Of course, Val had already had this imaginary argument with Kev, dozens of times. That was what she had hoped she'd be able to convince him of in this visit. She had thought these months apart would have been so miserable that he would agree. Now, she had to face the fact that in spite of all she'd said to him or written, in her letters, which he may or may not have read, he stayed stubbornly convinced that he was right in what he had demanded.

It was a complete rejection of everything Val had believed in. Kevin was trying to wipe out the past as though it had never happened, to deny their love as if it had never existed. She had been madly in love with Kevin, had rebelled against her loving parents in order to be with him. He had been the center of her life since high school. He and Megan had been her world.

Even in their darkest hour, when the missing funds were discovered and Kev told her he had taken the money, she had stood by him through the ordeal, suffering for him. She had never considered, even for a moment, running away from the disgrace, the nightmare of it. She had believed in those vows they had taken so long ago—"For better for worse…till death us do part." She could not easily give up her faith in their meaning.

Through the little grate in the stove, Val stared into the fire, watching the flames leap. Almost hypnotized by the dancing light, she seemed to hear a voice. *But isn't this a kind of death? Kevin is trying to kill your marriage, your love. When love dies, doesn't that end the marriage?*

After a while, Val stood up, went over to the window and looked out into the night. Far away, she could hear the roar of the surf crashing against the jetty. Suddenly, she was gripped by the idea of running out there, plunging into the sea and letting the waves wash over her, blotting out the hurt, the pain, the despair. She shuddered and turned back into the room. That was sick thinking. Self-destructive. *God forgive me.* Of course, there was Megan to think of, plan for, take care of. She was what was important. She and Kevin had brought her into the world. She was their responsibility. And now hers. Alone. She had no one to depend on. No one was going to rescue her. She had to be brave and resourceful. But most of all, she had to pray.

Val reported to The Seawinds an hour before her shift began in order to have time to take Megan to the sitter's. But Eileen McDermott took one look at her and ladled out a bowl of thick, creamy clam chowder and stood over Val while she ate every spoonful.

"No offense, Val, but you look like you could use some more time off. It must have been a grueling trip and certainly no picnic. Besides, Tom has taken Megan out fishing with him, so why don't you take the rest of the day off?" she suggested. "Colleen will be glad to take your shift. Only the other day she told me she'd welcome some extra hours. She's saving for college tuition in the fall. Okay?"

"That would be good," Val said gratefully. "Thanks, Mrs. McDermott."

"I think you can call me Eileen, Val." She patted Val's shoulder. "Most of the staff do, you know."

"Thanks, Eileen."

Relieved that Eileen had been sensitive enough not to probe for any details about her trip to see Kevin, Val promised to be in the next day as usual and left.

Back at the cottage, she changed from her uniform into some jeans and an old pullover and walked down to the beach. Deep in troubling thoughts, she walked without any real awareness of the direction and soon found herself out by the old stone jetty at the end. She went along the narrow stone path that jutted into the sea, feeling the salt spray from the dashing waves on her face. She sat down on the edge and tried to make sense of the visit, of what Kevin's mind-set was and what she should do now.

She realized how much their separation had changed her and how little Kevin's imprisonment had changed him. Oh, physically he had changed, but his basic character had not. He had a habit of rewriting facts, shaping them to his own benefit. After the awful disclosure of the embezzlement, Kev had gone through a period of maudlin self-pity. Normally a moderate drinker, he had begun to drink heavily those terrible days. He had wept, but not tears of repentance. Remorse, yes. And worst of all, he'd shifted the responsibility, rationalizing.

To Val's horror, he'd said over and over, "I did it for you, babe. You and Megan. I wanted to make a big financial killing. A lot of people I knew were getting rich. I had tips I thought were foolproof. I was going to make us secure for life."

Val hadn't contradicted him. What would have been

the use? He always knew better. Maybe she should have said, "Don't blame me, Kev. Blame yourself." But it seemed cruel to kick someone who was already down. Now she wished she had. Maybe she could have helped him see the truth.

She had to accept that Kevin meant it when he said he wanted them out of his life, that he wanted no reminders of a life that was over. When he got out of prison, whenever that happened, he wanted to make a fresh start on his own. Maybe she and Megan reminded him of his failure.

There was no point in looking back. No thinking about what might have been. No one could change the past. She had to build a new life without Kevin. For her own sake and especially for Megan's, and the sooner the better. Not just for the next few years but for the foreseeable future.

"It's over." She said the words with only the seagulls to hear. Somehow saying them out loud fortified her resolve. She took a deep breath and looked at the ocean. It was a dozen shades of blue, the sun scattering glittering lights like golden sequins on the rippling water.

She remembered that awful day after the court hearing in the hotel when she had, in desperation, sought help in the Gideon Bible. That same verse she'd looked up afterward in a Bible she'd found and bought in a thrift shop in town. She had often read it, seeking reassurance that she was not, after all, alone. Out of the chapter of Joshua the words, "I will be with you, I will not leave you or forsake you," came into her mind. If she could just believe that. Trust that promise. She would be okay.

The world was so beautiful. She was so blessed to be here, to be young, healthy, to have Megan. A spontaneous prayer of thanksgiving rose from Val's heart. She was really not alone.

Gradually, a kind of calm overtook her. The fog that had veiled her thinking slowly began to lift. The afternoon ebbed into the glow of the setting sun.

Val stood up and started back along the jetty and onto the beach toward their cottage. She felt a sadness for what had gone but a new hope about what might lie ahead. She lifted her head and started running. She was leaving her old life behind like her footprints in the sand. Soon the incoming tide would sweep in and all traces would disappear. A sense of confidence overtook her, the feeling that somehow things would work out....

PART II

Chapter Ten

The summer season was at its peak. The restaurant was crowded. Word of mouth about The Seawinds had resulted in more and more tourists "finding" it. Much of the increased business was due to an item that had appeared in a popular travel writer's column in the leisure section of the *San Francisco Chronicle*. Eileen had read it to the staff with a mixture of pride and surprise.

"'If you're in no hurry and want to meander down the coast and spend a delightful day having a delicious meal in a charming seaside restaurant with a spectacular ocean view, there's no better place than The Seawinds....'" With mock apprehension, Eileen said, "This may mean more work now that we're on the gourmet map."

It also meant the waitresses were paid overtime and the tips increased, which no one objected to and nobody minded. Colleen was going back to college in the fall and every extra penny Val earned was welcome.

Gradually, Val recovered from her experience visiting Kevin at the prison. She stopped thinking about how long it might take before Kev got out. For a long time, she couldn't get rid of that last image of him, his angry, sullen coldness toward her. Eventually the pain became bearable. It was no longer an open wound, raw and aching each day. Scar tissue was forming and slowly the healing process began.

In the fall, Megan would enter kindergarten. The doctors had told Val that until her deafness became so acute as to require special training in signing or lip-reading, it was thought better to "mainstream" the child in a regular school.

The Seawinds would close when the McDermotts went to Mexico, and although Val knew she had a job there when the restaurant reopened, she needed some income during the months they would be gone. She needed to find a temporary job. She didn't want to use up all her savings from the extra tips she'd earned at the height of the season. She would stay in the cottage, since there was no other place offering such reasonable rent. So Megan would be enrolled at Oceanview Elementary, in the next town over from Seawood.

In order to register her, Val had to produce Megan's birth certificate. It was when she was looking for it that Val came across her unsigned divorce papers. She had thrust away the folder with the accompanying letter from Brad Hensley because she could hardly bear the sight of it. Now, she took it out and reluctantly waded through all the legalese. Soon all the whereases and therefores started to blur. Impatiently, Val shoved the folder back into the drawer, making the excuse to herself that she'd review them some other time when she wasn't so rushed. Even as she told herself that, Val knew she was just putting off the inevitable. It just seemed so final. Once she signed those papers, there was no way back. It was the end of all hope. A hope that still lurked somewhere in the regions of her heart.

Labor Day weekend The Seawinds was booked solid. People were savoring the last days of summer vacation and every shift had tables filled to capacity. After that, the crowds gradually diminished and the staff breathed a collective sigh of relief. It had been a wonderfully successful launching of the restaurant and the McDermotts were already talking expansion. They had spoken to an architect about building on an addition and would probably spend their Mexican "vacation" making plans.

The season was coming to an end. The few renters of the other cottages had gone home, packing up their beach umbrellas, their plastic coolers, their Frisbees, beach balls and surfboards, leaving the beach deserted during the beautiful, long, sunny afternoons. Val realized she had gotten possessive about the beach and was glad to have it to herself again.

Megan, however, missed the children she had had a chance to play with during July and August. But when she started kindergarten she would soon have plenty of children to play with, Val reassured her. Val had taken Megan with her when she went to register her. She explained to the principal about Megan's hearing loss.

Mrs. Elwood listened sympathetically as Val told her that, according to the doctors, the deafness would be progressive but gradual. "Nowadays," she remarked, "it is considered best to mainstream children unless their disability is marked and would prevent them from participating or contributing in class." She glanced at Megan, who had been seated at a small table with a puzzle during the interview. "Your daughter seems bright and alert. I don't see any reason that would keep her from enjoying kindergarten. But I'd like you to meet her teacher and have a chance to talk to her about Megan."

She introduced Val to Miss Pierson, a young, pretty brunette with warm brown eyes and a wonderful smile. After a brief explanation, she began a short conversation with Megan, who responded with her usual spontaneity. Miss Pierson then turned to Val. "I don't see it as any problem."

"Megan's a very responsive little girl," Val volunteered. "I find if I speak directly to her, she has no difficulty. At a little distance, she doesn't always seem to hear me."

Miss Pierson nodded understandingly. "I'm sure it will work out just fine, Mrs. Madison. My sister's a special education teacher in southern California. I'll ask her if there are any suggestions she might have about later on." Then taking Megan's hand, she led her into the bright, cheerful kindergarten room, showed her all its colorful posters, the dollhouse, big building blocks, low round tables and little chairs, also modeling clay, even small easels for finger painting. Megan was very excited at the prospect of starting school and the experience had been a happy one.

From there they'd gone to the one department store in Oceanview where Val splurged on some new outfits for Megan. Then she let her pick out a lunchbox and a colorful padded rug for rest time and story hour. It was fun for both of them. However, on the first day Val took Megan to school, she was surprised at her mixed feelings. When she left her at the gate of the kindergarten playground she felt tears crowd into her eyes. Megan had gone happily into her new adventure. Yet for Val it seemed another letting go. Another page she was turning in life. Again, turning it alone.

Val walked back home on the beach instead of on the road. Along the California coast, the weather in autumn is often at its best. The days are bright and sunny but the mornings are usually cooler, with fog and the fog rolls in earlier and earlier in the afternoons.

As Val took the path off Beach Road over the dunes down to the beach, she was surprised to see smoke curling from the chimney of the cottage at the very end of the beach. It had remained empty all summer. Val had been so busy with work and getting Megan ready for school she had not noticed any activity down there. With the rest of the cottages empty, abandoned for the winter, it seemed strange to realize it was occupied.

A week went by, then two. The restaurant was now only open weekends. The staff was reduced, and Colleen, Val's closest friend among the waitresses, had left to go back to college. Val had applied and gotten a part-time clerking job at Murphy's hardware store in Seawood. Working mornings, Val had her afternoons free to be with Megan.

One day after work, she met Megan at the school bus stop and they went to have milkshakes before going grocery shopping. It was Friday, payday, and Val stocked up on canned goods. She didn't realize she had bought too much until she carried out two heavy bagloads and they started walking home.

They took the usual route, it had always seemed a shortcut, but now Val wished she'd stayed on the road.

The sun had suddenly disappeared, and a chill wind blew in from the ocean as they trudged along the water's edge.

Bent on getting home as quickly as possible, Val didn't notice Megan playing her favorite tag game with the incoming waves. That is, until Megan asked plaintively, "Can I take off my shoes, Mommy?"

Her arms aching from the heavy bags, Val turned around. "No, of course not. It's getting too cold to go barefoot."

It was then Val saw that Megan had got her canvas shoes soaked by walking too close to the water.

"Oh, Megan!" Val said sharply, feeling tired and cross. She could feel the edge of a can tearing through the bottom of one of the paper bags.

"But they feel all icky and they squoosh when I walk," Megan wailed.

"Well, that's too bad. You should have watched where you were walking and not gotten them wet." Val started walking again. "Now hurry up, the sooner we get home the sooner you can take off your shoes. Come on."

They continued on, Megan lagging behind. Val shifted the bags carefully, trying not to let the ripped one tear any more. But there was no stopping it. It fell completely apart and its contents—cans, cereal boxes, potatoes and apples—spilled out onto the sand.

"Oh, no! Megan, come help me!" Val called frantically, as she tried to catch a can of tomato juice rolling down toward the ocean.

Just then, a man seemed to appear out of nowhere, eerily emerging from the drifts of fog swirling around them. Val was too busy trying to retrieve her groceries even to register surprise.

"Can I help?" he asked.

She flung out her hands helplessly at the remnants of the paper bag, her scattered groceries. "Oh, please! I'm in a mess."

He began scooping up things randomly and setting them some distance from the incoming tide. "It looks like we caught everything before it got washed out to sea." Then, pointing in the direction of the last cottage on the beach, he said, "I'm staying over there. I could run up and get another bag for you or I could take you home in my car if you live around here."

Val glanced at him gratefully. "A bag would be a big help. I haven't far to go."

"If you're sure, then. I'll run up and get a bag. Be back in a jiff." She watched the tall figure sprint up the dunes and disappear into the cottage. So he was the mysterious renter.

There was something vaguely familiar about him. He had probably dined at The Seawinds sometime during the summer. She was trying to place him as one of the diners she might have served when he returned with a sturdy string bag.

Megan slipped her hand into Val's and asked in a stage whisper, "Why couldn't we take a ride, Mommy? I'm tired."

Val frowned and squeezed her hand warningly.

But the man had overheard her and smiled at Megan. "I'd be glad to give you a lift."

"No, thanks just the same. We live just down the

beach." Val pointed to their cottage, now dimly outlined in the thickening fog.

Efficiently, he placed all the groceries into the string
bag and slung it over his shoulder, saying, "I'll carry
this one for you. I was out for a walk anyway."

"That's very kind of you but—" Val began, but the
man just grinned and started walking.

"No problem," he said.

The wind off the ocean encouraged them all to
quicken their pace. Even Megan. Her attention was
fastened on the tall man who'd appeared out of the
fog. When they got to the wooden steps that led over
the dunes to the side of their cottage, Val stopped and
reached for the bag of groceries he had carried for her.
"Thank you very much."

"Not at all. By the way, since we are neigbors, I'm
Garth Hasten."

He didn't seem to notice Val's slight hesitation. After
his help it would have been rude not to introduce herself, too. "I'm Val Madison, and this is—"

But before she could finish, Megan was already introducing herself. "I'm Megan, I'm in kindergarten, the
morning session. Miss Pierson is my teacher and I can
tell time and tie my shoes and print my name."

"Megan," Val remonstrated gently.

But Garth laughed and said directly to Megan,
"That's wonderful."

"If you'll wait a minute, I'll empty this and give you
back your bag," Val said.

He dismissed the idea with a shake of his head. "No
need now. I can pick it up some other time. It was nice
meeting you." He took a few steps, then looked back

and said, "Well, so long, hope to see you both again soon." Then with a wave he continued down the beach.

Val stood there for a few seconds, watching the tall figure as he strode away. Maybe she should have asked him in for a cup of coffee after he had come to their rescue and been so helpful. But what would she possibly have to talk to him about? What would they have in common?

From the look of his expensively casual clothes, the stonewashed jeans, the cable-knit sweater, his reasons for renting one of these cheap cottages were not the same economic ones as hers. No, it would have been awkward if she asked him in.

"Come on, Megan," she said, and with Megan wearily trailing behind in her soggy canvas shoes, they went up the rickety wooden steps and into the house.

When she let herself in, the house seemed particularly empty, depressing in an odd, indefinable way.

Megan plopped herself down on the floor and began tugging at her wet shoes, complaining, "I don't see why we couldn't take a ride."

"Because I've told you over and over we never accept rides from strangers." Val spoke with exaggerated patience.

"But he wasn't a stranger. He's our neighbor," Megan replied. Val glanced at the little girl. She started to explain further, then decided that to Megan her reasoning made perfect sense. Instead, she just said, "Go change your socks, honey, and I'll make us some cocoa."

Val busied herself in the kitchen. But as she started putting away the groceries, she felt an unexpected urge to cry. How stupid, she thought, biting her lip. She suddenly felt an aching loneliness. Why? Because someone had been kind to her, helped her? In the past months, she had learned to do so many things because she'd had no one else to depend on, but she was tired. She longed for what she dared not admit she missed—someone to lean on, someone to care about her....

From Megan's room, she heard the tinny sound of the little hand-cranked record player they'd found in a thrift shop along with some story records. Megan had learned to do without television and playmates after school. She had adjusted to their new life. Why couldn't *she?*

After Megan was asleep in bed, Val determinedly got out the speed-writing book she'd written away for from an ad she'd seen in a magazine. Someday she might need to look for a better-paying job to support them. An office job. Later, if Megan needed special tutoring or had to attend a special school for the deaf, it might cost a great deal. She had to think ahead. No one else was around to depend on but herself. Sure, Megan was only in kindergarten now, but time went fast and she should be prepared.

For some reason, Val found it hard to concentrate that evening. Her mind tended to drift off to that chance encounter with the neighbor. There was something about him... The eyes? The smile? He seemed genuinely kind and friendly. But Val couldn't afford the luxury of friendship.

Finally, she gave up trying to study and went to bed. Yet she was restless. There were many nights, even when she was really tired, that she couldn't sleep. She'd lie there, tense, as though waiting, listening... For what? The step that never came, the laughter of a shared joke, the warmth of companionship. That night, the loneliness she usually kept at bay seemed painfully intense.

In the last cottage down the beach, the kerosene lamp burned brightly. Garth Hasten was busily setting up his work space. He'd been out of the country for several months and only been back in the States a couple of days. He'd wasted no time but driven down from San Francisco eager to get to his beach studio. He was energized in spite of the fact he should be experiencing jet lag.

Everything was just as he'd left it months before. His drawing table, placed in the front room at the windows, had a view of the beach and ocean. Meticulously, he set out his brushes, his paints, checked his stacks of sketchbooks on the shelves built under the windows. He was full of enthusiasm and anticipation. But he knew it would take him days to settle in enough to really work.

Idly, he picked up one of his sketchbooks at random and glanced quickly through it to see if any of his sketches would be usable for this new project. He discarded it and picked up another, noting the date on the cover. He always dated his sketchbooks, noted where and when he'd used them. San Francisco, almost a year ago. He started turning the pages, then lingered at one. A woman's face. Ghirardelli Square, the rooftop restaurant, a brilliant fall day, the sun on the Bay, the Chinese kites against the vivid blue sky. He studied the sketch. He'd done it rapidly, no time for details, just an impression. But he had caught something in her expression, something that had remained with him for a long time afterward. Since then, of course, he'd done hundreds of other sketches. He'd almost forgotten her. Until today. The woman on the beach.

At first glance, he wasn't certain about her, but he was sure it was the same little girl. He had not forgotten the child who he'd thought would be perfect for his Goldilocks illustration. The woman, however, looked different now, thinner, her hair a darker brown and cut casually short.

He thought back to the day he had first seen them both. The woman of his sketch had the aloof blond-goddess look of Grace Kelly. Dressed simply but expensively with understated good taste. Her dark glasses had given her an aura of glamour, mystery. But when she had taken them off, her eyes, gray, shadowed by dark lashes, had looked…haunted?

He had started to say something today on the beach. Haven't we met before? Too clichéd. He had stopped himself. It was foolish to think she would have remembered him. Their encounter had been awkward. He had acted impulsively, asking her for permission to use the little girl as a model. Naturally, she'd been suspicious, protective of her child. He'd been coolly refused, he remembered ruefully. Dismissed, actually.

But what were they doing here, in this out-of-the-way beach town, living in one of these isolated cottages?

There was some story there. Something must have happened to bring them to this place. He was curious and he still would like to paint the child.

Surely their paths would cross again. It seemed too much of a coincidence not to be significant. Maybe they'd become friends. Anything was possible.

Chapter Eleven

The following Saturday, Val and Megan took a picnic to their special cove. It was a perfect day. The cove was sheltered from the wind and there was a sandbar that stretched far out so that Megan could play safely in the water that curved into the sandy beach.

Megan was a child of the sea. She was never happier than when she was at the beach, building roads and tunnels in the sand, running back and forth with her bucket. Val had brought along her speed-writing manual, thinking she would practice. However, after a few distracted moments, it lay in her lap unread. The ocean was too beguiling, with its ebb and flow, providing her endless fascination. She was lazily daydreaming when suddenly she heard Megan saying, "Hi."

Startled, she raised her head to see Garth Hasten, the rescuer in the grocery disaster. She immediately felt a twinge of guilt. She had not as yet returned his string bag. She had no excuse, she had just put off taking it back. She tried to think of what to say. At the moment, he was squatting on his heels beside Megan, looking with interest at the castle she was building, giving her his complete attention.

There's a man who loves children. The thought flashed through Val's mind. Not everyone knew how to interact with them, but this man did. Even as she was thinking this, he stood up, turned and smiled at her. Then, accompanied by Megan, he walked toward her. He was carrying a fishing rod, and a well-worn creel was slung by a leather strap over one shoulder.

"Hi there, Mrs. Madison," he greeted her. "I've had some real luck this morning. Could you use some fresh fish for dinner tonight? I've got way more than I can possibly eat."

Fresh-caught fish were a treat anytime. Val's grocery budget, usually limited to basic staples, rarely included such delicacies. Even at the risk of becoming more indebted to this man, it would have seemed rude to refuse his generous offer.

Evidently mistaking her hesitation for something else, he grinned. "They're all cleaned. All they need is to be dipped in a little egg and cornmeal, some butter and a hot frying pan."

"You must be quite a cook," Val managed to say.

"Bachelors have to be or they'd starve." He laughed. "So, how about it?"

"Well, yes, thank you, that's very generous of you."

"Good, I'm on my way home. I'll put these in some ice and bring them over later."

Uh-oh, Val thought, watching him walk away. Did that mean she'd have to ask him in? She didn't want to start anything with this stranger, handsome and congenial though he seemed to be. It would just complicate her already complicated life.

She purposely lingered down at the cove longer than usual, telling herself it was because Megan was having such a good time and the day was so warm, so beautiful. Actually, she was avoiding another encounter with Garth Hasten that might prove awkward.

At last it was time to pack up. When they got to their cottage, on their porch was a small plastic container with the fish packed in ice. On it was a note. "Enjoy, GH." To her own chagrin, Val felt a small pang of disappointment to have missed him.

That evening, they had the delicious fish for supper. Later, when the dishes were washed and put away, Val settled down to read Megan her bedtime story. It was a familiar one that Megan often requested and Val found her mind wandering even as she spoke the words. Her feelings about their new neighbor were mixed. In one way, she was drawn to him; in another, she was leery of becoming too friendly. It was Megan who made a surprising statement that caused Val to rethink her attitude.

As she was getting ready to say her prayers before getting into bed, the little girl said, "I think I'll add our neighbor to my God-blesses tonight, Mommy. He's nice, isn't he?"

"Yes, he is, honey," Val answered. Afterward, she thought Megan was right. Garth Hasten had been nothing but cordial and helpful. Why did she feel somehow threatened by his entrance into their lives?

It wasn't until a week later that Val saw Garth Hasten again. Every time she noticed his string bag hanging on the hook by the kitchen door, she reminded herself she must return it. Somehow she felt shy about doing so.

"I'll wait until a day when Megan is with me and we're walking into town," Val promised herself aloud. "I really must do it before he stops here, asks for it." Although that seemed unlikely, the thought of Garth Hasten's towering figure arriving at her cottage door was unnerving. His appearance was so masculine, his manner so self-assured. Silly as it seemed, she didn't want to encourage an acquaintanceship with their attractive neighbor.

A week went by. Almost every day, Val saw Garth Hasten walk past her cottage. Sometimes he had fishing gear with him; other times he just strolled leisurely along the ocean's edge. She was tempted to run outside, return his string bag. But then she hung back. She didn't want him to know she often stood at her window, half-hidden by the curtain, and watched him go by. She had succeeded in cocooning herself all these months, keeping her real identity a secret, not inviting even the staff at The Seawinds to be friends. It was safer that way.

As it turned out, she ran into him again purely by accident. She had taken Megan to catch the school bus and was walking back to the cottage along the beach. It was a beautiful morning, the sky clear, the sun bright, the ocean deep blue, the air tangy with salt. As she went along, she was thinking how lucky, in spite of the circumstances that had brought them to this spot, they were to live here. More like, blessed, she amended. More and more she had come to believe that God had directed her steps, just as she had prayed that desperate day after Kevin's sentencing.

"Mrs. Madison." At the sound of her name, Val whirled around and saw Garth Hasten striding up the beach behind her. She halted to let him catch up with her. "You're out early, too, I see," he said. "Mind if I keep you company?" Without waiting for an answer, he just started walking alongside her. "Boy, what a great day? Look at those whitecaps. We're sure having some weather, aren't we? The best I've ever seen this time of year and I've been coming down here every fall for years."

That caught Val's attention. Why had he chosen this particular beach? Val couldn't guess.

He talked easily, unselfconsciously. "I feel so alive here. There's something special about this place, don't you agree? Unspoiled." He glanced over at her as if for confirmation.

Knowing her reasons were far different from his, Val didn't answer. Garth didn't seem to notice, just went on talking, saying he'd gotten up at dawn, walked down to the dock, ate breakfast with some of the fishermen.

Finally, they neared the place where she usually cut over the dunes to her own cottage and she halted. "I still have the string bag you lent me. Would you wait here a minute while I run up and get it?"

"There's no hurry. You can stop by any time you and Megan are out and bring it over."

Val hesitated. "Well, if you're sure?"

"Yes, any time. I'm usually there. Well, so long." With that, Garth went on down the beach.

Val climbed the rickety wooden steps leading to her cottage. As she went inside, Val was irritated with herself. Garth Hasten must think her a real dud. *What's the matter with me? I can't even carry on a decent conversation. I never used to be like this.* Of course, she knew it was because of the awful events that had changed her life forever. Wouldn't she ever get over it, be normal again?

A few days later, before walking Megan to the bus stop, she folded the string bag and stuck it in her jacket pocket, intending to make a quick stop at Garth Hasten's cottage on her way home. If he wasn't there, she could easily leave it wedged into the screen door. She wouldn't have to knock or anything, just leave it there, she told herself. Then felt annoyed by all this fuss. Why was she making such a big deal about such an ordinary errand?

The wind off the ocean was brisk and she walked with her head down, bent against it. That's how she happened not to see Garth coming from the other direction.

He greeted her with his usual good humor. Taken by surprise, she stammered, "I—I was just coming by your place to—"

"Good!" He didn't let her finish. "How about coming in and having a cup of coffee? I just made a pot and while it was brewing came out looking around for some driftwood."

Val knew it would be stupid to refuse. Still, she paused uncertainly.

Garth said in a gently teasing voice, "I won't bite, I promise. I've been down here for three weeks and I haven't had any company at all. I just walked to town and bought some fresh bagels. Please come and share them."

His smile was so genuine, his voice so friendly, Val realized it would look silly not to accept his invitation. After all, as Megan had pointed out, they were neighbors.

Inside Garth's cottage, Val looked around with interest. It had exactly the same floor plan as hers, but it was decorated in a unique style. All along one side of the front room, there were built-in bookcases filled with books, shells, odd pieces of driftwood. Then she saw the drawing table at the windows.

"Why, you're an artist!" she said, turning to look at him with a mixture of awe and surprise.

"Yes."

She looked at two framed seascapes, then at a stack of unframed canvases stacked against the wall. "Are those yours?"

"Yes."

"Why didn't you tell me you were an artist?" she asked. "It seems like something you'd tell someone right away."

"Maybe. Sometimes it puts people off." He paused and looked at her skeptically. "Should I have told you?" He grinned. "Maybe if I had, you wouldn't have come here. You know the old line that goes, 'I'd like to show you my etchings.' In my case, my sketches." He gave her a teasing look. "You wouldn't have come, would you?"

She had to laugh. "Oh, I don't know, maybe not. But it's wonderful. To be talented, I mean."

"Everyone is talented in one way or another. Mine just happens to be my livelihood."

"How marvelous to be able to work at something you love."

"Don't you?"

Val shrugged. "I'm a waitress at The Seawinds. It's not exactly what you'd call a talent."

"That depends. I've had some great waitresses and some surly ones. It certainly makes a difference to the enjoyment of a meal."

Garth went into the small kitchen area at the end of the main room. Val heard the clatter of cups, of cabinet doors opening and closing. She went to look out the window. "You have a fantastic view from here."

"Sure do. On a clear day I can see past the jetty, out to the lighthouse." He came out from the counter divider bringing an aluminum coffee carafe. "Come sit over here at this window. There's another view down to the end of the beach. I can see your cottage from here, just at the curve of the inlet."

She sat down at the scrubbed oak table in the alcove. Sure enough, she could see their small weathered cottage behind the dunes. In a few minutes, Garth brought a tray to the table, set down pottery mugs and a basket of bagels, a jar of marmalade and a crock of butter.

Val took a sip of the delicious coffee. "Mmm, this is wonderful. Freshly ground, gourmet, right? I've forgotten how good real coffee tastes. I use instant since I'm the only one who drinks—" She stopped abruptly. She hadn't meant to say something like that, give away her single status so quickly.

Garth picked up on it immediately. He stirred sugar into his coffee, looking at her directly. "Then there's no Mr. Madison?"

Val felt breathless as she always did when she had to hedge the truth. She took another sip of coffee before answering in a low voice, "No."

"Actually, that's what I've been trying to find out. Hoping to find out. I mean, I've seen you and Megan a lot. Even before we officially met. Remember the grocery fiasco?" He smiled broadly. "I've seen you walking by. Then that day on the beach. Naturally, I couldn't help wonder. I mean, obviously Megan had to have a father. What I guess I'm trying to ask is would it be okay for me to ask you to go out with me sometime?" Val's shock must have shown on her face. Garth put down his coffee, his expression all concern. "Sorry. Did I say something out of line?"

She shook her head. "No, not at all. It's just that I haven't been going out—yet."

"I should have asked first. Are you divorced, or is he...dead?"

Later, much later, Val was to remember her moment of truth. Or rather, untruth. At the time, it hadn't seemed that important. After all, everyone at The Seawinds, except Eileen and Tom, thought she was separated. But, right then, as Garth's steady gaze held hers, she had felt trapped. Still, he was someone she'd really just met. He'd told her he was only staying until December. After that, he would leave Seawood. She'd never see him again. What difference did it make?

Besides, Kevin might as well be dead. That's the way he wanted it, wasn't it? In that split second of decision, Val justified her answer.

"He's dead."

"Has it been long?" Garth asked next.

"Almost a year," she said tightly, wishing desperately she'd never come here for coffee, never gotten into this whole mess. It would be rude to get up and leave at this point. Escape. Common courtesy required her to finish her coffee, carry on some kind of conversation. She glanced at Garth and saw that he was looking so anxious she felt sorry for him.

"I'm sorry. I shouldn't have asked. Forgive me. I always seem to be starting out on the wrong foot with you."

"What do you mean?" she asked, puzzled.

"You don't remember, do you?" Garth paused. "San Francisco, about this time last year. The rooftop restaurant at Ghirardelli Square. I asked if you would allow Megan to model for me. I'm the artist who did the sketch of her."

Val put down her mug and stared at him. Slowly, the incident floated back into her memory. Of course, the sketch of Megan, the bearded man who had come to their table.

"That was *you?*" she demanded. "But you don't look the same."

Garth rubbed his jaw. "I've shaved off my beard."

Val scrutinized him. "Yes, now I vaguely…" Her voice faded as a more vivid memory took its place. That was the day—the terrible day—she had learned what Kevin had done. Everything else that happened that day had simply disappeared. Except for that one awful reality. No wonder she hadn't recognized Garth Hasten.

"Look, I don't know how to apologize," Garth said. "Maybe I should have told you right away, that first day I met you on the beach. Told you who I was and that I recognized you…well, actually, I recognized Megan first." He paused. "You've changed a little yourself."

Self-consciously, Val touched her hair. "Yes, I know.

I wore my hair differently then." She spoke slowly through stiff lips. Her voice seemed to be coming from a long way off. It was such a strange, fantastic coincidence.

"It's none of my business, I know, but why are you living here? Seawood is a long way from Marin."

"I wanted to get away from things. Make a new start," Val said. That at least was the unvarnished truth.

"But I've heard when you lose someone you love, you need the support. Is it a good idea to isolate yourself from people who care, could help, and live so far from family and friends?"

"There is no family, nor any friends." Val's mouth twisted slightly. "No people who care."

"No one?" He stared at her, making Val feel even more uncomfortable. "That's hard to believe."

"Believe it," Val said, and stood up. "I really have to go. Lots to do before time to meet Megan."

He walked with her to the door and opened it for her. "Look, have I messed up things impossibly between us or can we be…friends? I'd like that very much."

"Of course."

"I'd really hate it if I've offended you. I didn't mean to."

"It's all right, really." He was blocking her way out and she wanted to leave badly. It had been a mistake to come here. She'd talked too much, told this man too much. He moved away, giving her room to pass.

"I have to go up to the city for a few days on business. But when I come back, could I see you, make some plans?"

"I don't know." Val began to feel suffocated. She had to get out of here.

"I'll call, then, may I?" he persisted.

"I don't have a phone. I really have to go," she said, and stepped out onto the porch. "Thanks for the coffee," she said over her shoulder, then hurried down his wooden path, over the dunes and onto the beach, without looking back.

Chapter Twelve

Val was breathless when she reached her cottage. Hurrying inside, she shut the door behind her and leaned against it feeling suddenly dizzy. After all she'd done to conceal her identity, her past, her careful cover had been blown. Garth Hasten had recognized her. This man, of all people, to come to this out-of-the-way place. It was unbelievable.

She closed her eyes for a minute. The details of that day that she'd pushed to the back of her mind now came rushing back in agonizing detail. Taking Megan to the specialist in the city and receiving the bad prognosis. Then later, the revelation from Kevin about the embezzlement. It had been the worst day of her life. She wanted to forget it forever. Now, it was impossible.

She had forgotten all about that incident with Garth Hasten in the restaurant. And here he was in Seawood. Wanting to be friends.

All during the next week, Val ventured out very little. The weather turned gray and foggy. That was excuse enough not to go down to the beach. Of course, her real reason was to avoid Garth Hasten. When she walked up to meet Megan's bus, she went along the sea-wall instead of the beach.

Sometimes when she was standing at the window facing the ocean, she would see him striding along the edge of the water. Often he seemed to slow his walk below their cottage and look up. Her heart strangely pounding, Val would step back so as not to be seen. Then he'd walk on. He never came up to the cottage door.

When a few days went by and she didn't see him Val recalled he had told her he was going up to the city. She missed seeing the lights in the cottage at the far end of the inlet. It made her feel lonelier than ever, more isolated.

Then, one Friday night at the end of her shift, Eileen asked Val to take over the register. She had a long-distance call from her daughter back east and wanted to talk to her. Val was just adding up some receipts when a familiar voice asked, "Good evening, Mrs. Madison."

Val looked up. It was Garth Hasten. "You're back!"

He was wearing a tweed jacket, button-down shirt, a great-looking tie. He looked very handsome. "Is it too late to be served?"

"No, I don't think so...." She felt two things at once—unexpected pleasure at seeing him and a concern that she might show it.

Just at that moment, Eileen came out of her office and saw Garth. "Garth Hasten!" she exclaimed. "What a happy surprise!"

"Hi, Eileen," he greeted her. "Where's Tom?"

"Watching TV, but wait until I tell him you're here." She turned to Val. "We knew Garth in San Francisco when we had our restaurant there. He was one of our favorite customers." She looked back at Garth. "I guess you've been holed up in your beach place painting, haven't you? It really is great to see you." Again she turned to Val. "Why don't you show Garth to a table and I'll tell Johnny."

"You brought Johnny down here with you?" Garth said in surprise. "No wonder you're on the map. You've been written up in the *Chronicle*." To Val, he explained, "Johnny's one of the best chefs in northern California."

"Will it be sole or salmon, then?" Eileen asked.

"Sole will be great, thanks, Eileen." When Eileen went in search of her husband and to place a dinner order for Garth, he turned a disconcertingly direct gaze on Val. "And how have you been? And how is Megan?"

"Fine, fine. We're both fine," she answered, feeling her face warm, her heart beating faster. She fastened the receipts with a paperclip and placed them in the register drawer, realizing her hands were shaking a little.

Garth leaned his elbows on the counter beside the register and said, "I missed you. You and Megan."

Val looked at him, wondering if her expression gave her away, revealed that she had missed him, too. But Tom came in at that moment and greeted Garth heartily. While the two men were talking, Val slipped out through the kitchen, got her jacket from the employees' lounge and left.

She hurried down the road to the sitter's house to pick up Megan. It was irrational to rush out like that, but she had not wanted to linger at The Seawinds.

She had been taken aback by Garth's sudden appearance, even more by her own reaction to seeing him again. His obvious interest in her was unnerving. There wasn't room in her life for anyone else. She had all she could handle.

Later, after Megan was tucked in, Val went to the window in the front room and looked out. There were lights in the last cottage. It was then Val realized she had missed Garth Hasten and she was glad he was back in Seawood.

The next day was Saturday, a cold gray morning. Megan was happy, excited because today she had been invited to spend the day with a friend from her kindergarten class. Ever since school started, she had talked endlessly about a little girl named Bonnie. "We're best friends," she had announced almost from the first day.

At the open house for parents, Bonnie's mother, seeing Val with Megan, introduced herself. "I'm Chris Faraday, and you must be Megan's mom. I guess you know our girls are inseparable. I wonder if you'd allow Megan to come spend the day with Bonnie next Saturday? I couldn't find a phone listing for you or I'd have called. I thought I might take them to lunch and to Playland Park?"

Val felt the urgent tug on her hand and looked down into Megan's upturned eager face. She had overheard the invitation. While she'd resisted making friends herself, she knew she couldn't deprive Megan of the normal pleasures of childhood or keep her in the prison *she* had created for herself. No matter what, Megan had to have her own life. So permission was given and plans made. The two little girls were ecstatic.

Saturday morning, Val walked with Megan up to the service station on the highway above the beach where they had arranged for Mrs. Faraday to pick her up. That had been Val's idea. She felt self-conscious about anyone coming to their shabby little cottage. She was ashamed of feeling that way, knowing it was false pride. However, Mrs. Faraday reminded Val of her former neighbors in Meadowbrook; she was well-groomed in the casual style of young California suburbanites. Val still wasn't comfortable with her present situation in comparison with the life she had lived before. The life Chris Faraday was probably living.

The Faradays' shiny station wagon was waiting. Mrs. Faraday had a friend with her who was going along. She introduced her, then told Megan to hop in the back seat with Bonnie, and with a wave they drove off. Val stood watching the station wagon disappear down the road, feeling suddenly deserted. That was the sort of thing she and Emily used to do together. Pack the kids in the car and take off for a day at the zoo or park or beach. For a few minutes, Val felt the desperate longing for a friend, for an afternoon lunching or shopping at the mall. It had been so long since she'd done anything frivolous or simply fun.

She turned to start walking back to the cottage. Fog was drifting up from the beach so that even the ocean was blocked from view. It felt depressing. Val wondered how she would fill the hours ahead today without Megan's cheerful little presence.

She thrust her hands into her jacket pockets and headed down the sandy hill. Thinking of the day ahead alone was bad enough, but that thought dragged up the bleak picture of the years ahead. A lifetime ahead.

Val wasn't sure how long she'd been walking, lost in

her dreary thoughts, when she saw the dim outline of a figure moving toward her. The beach was deserted. Val threw a quick look over her shoulder. No one else was in sight. The sounds from the highway behind her were muted by the dense fog. For the first time since she had moved here, Val felt a clammy fear slide over her. She stopped. The urge to turn and run in the opposite direction was strong. But she wasn't sure exactly where she was in relation to her cottage. The figure moved steadily closer. As it came nearer, she let out a sigh of relief. She recognized the man breaking through the swirling mist.

It was Garth Hasten. Her relief was rapidly replaced by a flash of embarrassment. She remembered that she had run out of the restaurant the other evening without even saying goodbye. He must think her terribly rude.

When he was about five feet away, he greeted her jovially, "Well, if it isn't my neighbor, the elusive Mrs. Madison. All these sunny afternoons we've had lately, I've looked for you and Megan on the beach, but you were a no-show. Now, here you come out of the fog."

She couldn't think of anything to say to that. Although his voice had a teasing quality, Val guessed from the expression on his face that he knew the truth that she had been avoiding him. For a minute, the roar of the unseen ocean and the harsh cries of the gulls were the only sounds in the awkward silence that fell between them. Val fumbled with the zipper on her jacket, then pulled the hood up over her head, shivering in the wind.

"Looks like we're the only ones braving it out today," Garth said, "except for the gulls. Of course, they're foraging for food. Which isn't a bad idea. I was just going in search of some myself. It's a perfect day for a bowl of clam chowder. Would you and Megan join me?"

"Megan's gone for the day. To lunch with friends in Oceanview."

"Then why don't you come along? Since we're both on our own. I don't like eating alone, do you?" He smiled and took a few steps to come beside her. He took her arm and turned her around. "Besides, I'd enjoy the company. I've been holed up alone most of the week and it's getting to me." He laughed, and before she realized it, they were walking together toward the fishing dock.

Half an hour later, sitting opposite Garth at a table in the steamy dockside diner, spooning delicious, thick, creamy chowder, Val wondered why she had resisted. There was a warm, friendly atmosphere here. Voices and laughter of the commercial fishermen and the "regulars" provided a pleasant background. Her uncertainty about going with him soon disappeared. Garth's casual, forthright manner made being with him easy.

He told her he had been seeing people in San Francisco related to his art business, and now that all that had been taken care of, he had to settle down to the real work.

"It's all very well being taken out to dinner, complimented on the last book I did and picking up a few royalty checks. Now I have to produce. You're only as good as your last book."

"I've seen some of your work," Val said shyly. "At Megan's kindergarten there are several of the books you've illustrated. Megan happens to love the one about Petey, the squirrel who lives in the tree outside Buddy

Bascombe's house and observes all that goes on inside from his little hole."

"Well, how about that." Garth seemed genuinely pleased and surprised. "I did that one at least five years ago. So it's still around?"

"And being read and loved by children. You should feel proud."

"I do. It's very rewarding to know something you do makes someone happy."

"How did you get started as an illustrator? I mean, it must be very difficult to get assignments, isn't it?"

"Yes, until you have a track record. You have to serve an apprenticeship. Get known, recognized. Then it's also luck. Hard work. I peddled my portfolio for a number of years before I got my first real break. I did lots of other things in the meantime before what I'm doing now. Worked for an advertising agency. Hated it. I like being on my own. Choosing my own work."

He paused. "I had a mentor. Actually, two. One of my art teachers thought I had promise. And his wife. They took me under their wings. Angel wings." He laughed. "Fed me a lot of times when I probably would have gone hungry. Saw me through the disappointments. Millie, that's Don's wife, was particularly wonderful. She had a saying, 'When one door closes, another opens.' I've found that to be true. You never know what's in store for you around the next corner. No matter how you plan your life."

Val thought she could say amen to that. If Garth had any idea how her life had changed, turned upside down, he'd be even more convinced of what he was saying.

Afterward, Val couldn't remember how long they remained there talking. The waitress came, refilled their coffee mugs several times, but they were scarcely aware of it. Of course, it was Garth who did most of the talking. He seemed to realize this. "I'm sorry, I've been talking your ear off, haven't I? You must think I'm a complete egotist." His smile was somewhat sheepish. "And I really want to know about you. That must be pretty obvious. I've been hoping for a chance like this. Just to spend some time with you, reassure you. Whatever impression you may have gotten. I'm really quite harmless."

Val laughed. "I know."

"Yes, but that first time I *was* pretty brash, presumptuous, asking you to let Megan model for me."

"First impressions can often be wrong," Val said, smiling.

"My first impression of you wasn't wrong." Garth looked serious. "I thought you were beautiful, charming and somehow mysterious."

"Mysterious?" Val felt the color flow into her face.

"Yes, as if—" But Garth didn't get to finish whatever he was about to say because the waitress came with the check. It was a welcome interruption for Val. They were treading on dangerous territory.

They walked back along the slate gray beach. Coming from the other direction, his cottage was the first one in the row. They stopped just below it and stood there for a few minutes.

"Would you like to come up for a while, toast your toes in front of my fire? The afternoon is still young." His eyes were hopeful.

Val knew Megan wouldn't be back until after five.

It was tempting, but she decided it wasn't a good idea. She could imagine the intimate setting, shut off by the fog, sitting together in front of the Franklin stove, the conversation perhaps verging off into the more personal. No, it was dangerous. Too dangerous.

Val shook her head. "No, thanks, I better get home. I have a lot of catching up kind of things to do this weekend. Then I have to go meet Megan."

Garth looked disappointed but not defeated. He insisted on walking with her to her cottage. At the door, he said, "Maybe, you could come and bring Megan another time? She'd probably enjoy seeing the original paintings of some of the illustrations she might have seen in the books you mentioned."

"Yes, I'm sure she'd love that," Val said, thinking how considerate and sensitive of him to include Megan. "Well, thanks for a really enjoyable afternoon."

"Thank you for coming." Garth took her hand and held it for a minute. Again, he seemed to be about to say something more. Evidently he thought better of it and instead said, "Be seeing you. Tell Megan 'hi' for me." Then he went whistling down the boardwalk and the fog closed behind him.

Val went inside. She felt happy and also vulnerable. She had enjoyed the unexpected afternoon with Garth Hasten, maybe more than was safe.

Chapter Thirteen

Without Val's fully realizing it, that day spent with Garth marked a definite turning point for her. It was as if a burden had been lifted and she could take a deep breath. She had been afraid to let her guard down, to be close to people, fearing it might endanger her careful plan to hide from the past. But the more time she spent with Garth, the more comfortable she became.

It happened so naturally—the chance meetings on the beach, the walks, the conversations, the times he joined her and Megan on sunny afternoons at the cove. Over the next few weeks, Garth Hasten became a part of their life. For the first time in months, Val discovered that she woke up in the morning not dreading but looking forward to the day.

He was true to his promise of having Megan and Val over. One Friday afternoon, they came home to find a card from Garth stuck in their screen door. It was painted with his own artwork; clowns and cats and pumpkins were scattered in profusion along the border of an invitation for them to come to lunch on Saturday.

"Can we, Mommy, can we go?" Megan asked, jumping up and down with excitement. Val had told her what Garth did. Megan had used her *Petey the Squirrel* book for her show-and-tell day at kindergarten, proudly announcing that the man who had done the pictures was her neighbor.

Upon arriving at his cottage, Val saw that Garth had gone to a great deal of trouble. He had decorated the table with colorful mats and used bright Fiesta china. He had prepared food that any child would love—hamburgers on buns, French fries, a platter of finger-size crisp veggies, a creamy dip, large tossed salad with chocolate cake for dessert. He spent time showing Megan his paintings, then opened a large trunk filled with stuffed animals, rag dolls, wooden toys of various kinds, the props he used in his illustrations. She was in a child's wonderland.

Leaving her to explore the contents, Garth went over to Val, who'd been watching them. "Megan is really special, Val. She's so bright. She's unusually attentive. She listens so intently to everything I'm saying."

Val hesitated, then decided why not. "Garth, one explanation may be that she has impaired hearing." He looked startled, so she went on, "The reason she listens so carefully is so she won't miss anything. When we were first told about her loss of normal hearing, the doctors suggested that we speak very slowly and distinctly to her. When she was little, I used to hold her face by her chin and be sure that I had eye contact before I spoke."

"I'm sorry. I would never have guessed." Garth turned to glance at Megan, who was having the time of her life with two puppets. "It must have been a blow to you and your husband when you found out."

Val remembered Kevin's reaction—anger, bitterness, blaming God. She thrust the memory away, trying not to shudder. It had seemed so inappropriate at the time. When she'd tried to talk to him about it, he'd become even angrier.

Garth was looking at her expectantly.

"Yes, it was," she answered.

"Can something be done, an operation?"

"No, they don't suggest that. Just to be prepared as the loss becomes more acute. Later, we may start her signing. But people who lose their hearing after they have their language, who've heard sounds, voices, music, the normal noises of life, have a much easier time learning to read lips, speak."

There was a look of such compassion in Garth's eyes that Val almost wanted to confide in him more. It was so comforting to talk about Megan, how wonderful it would be to share her anxieties, her concerns about her future. But that would be a mistake. To confide all that would only weaken her. Garth was just passing through her life. In a few months, he would be gone and she'd still have to carry on alone.

This all went through Val's mind in seconds. Before she could fully absorb the meaning, Megan came over to her with the picture she had been coloring while Val and Garth talked. As she always did when she wanted Val's undivided attention, Megan thrust the paper right in front of Val's face and tapped on her knee at the same time.

"Look, Mommy, look. See, I drew a picture of our house." Val took the paper and held it out so she could see it better. Megan had drawn a house with a deck, a gray-haired woman standing beside the front door and a little girl playing with a dog in the yard. A car was in the driveway and two other figures, a man and a woman, were standing beside it. At once, Val felt a chill. It was their house in Meadowbrook, not the little beach cottage. At the same time, Val was conscious that Garth was leaning over her shoulder also looking at the drawing.

"That's very good, Megan," he said. "It really is, Val."

Megan looked pleased at his comment. Then a small frown puckered her brow and she asked earnestly, "When is Daddy going to come get us? It's been a long time."

Something cold and hard clutched Val's heart. All she had ever told Megan was that Daddy had had to go away for a while, maybe a very long time. Caught in the lie she'd told Garth, she felt trapped. Her mouth went dry. Megan rarely mentioned Kevin even though he was always in her God-blesses at prayer time. Val assumed she had forgotten that there ever had been another life in Meadowbrook until here in her drawing were all the missing pieces of that life—Harriet, Flynn and Kevin.

It was Garth who saved the moment. "Is that your dog? What's his name?" It switched Megan's focus immediately.

"Yeah, that's Flynn. But I didn't draw him very good. He's big and brown and black and his coat is really rough."

"Dogs are hard to get right. I have trouble with them myself," Garth said. "Come on, I'll show you an easy way to draw one." He got up and led Megan over to his drawing table, and for the next half hour, they were busily involved drawing dogs.

Weak with relief that the sticky moment had passed, Val felt grateful for Garth's instinctive tact. However, she wondered if, or more likely when, Garth might ask her if Megan did not know her father was dead.

Chapter Fourteen

Even though Val didn't feel she could confide fully all the circumstances of her life to Garth, she decided to appreciate his friendship while he was staying in Seawood. Val knew that friendship was all it was, and all it ever would be. Since Garth seemed to accept these unspoken limits and never tried to push their relationship beyond casual companionship, Val relaxed.

The pleasant autumn weather lingered, and they spent happy hours on the still-sunny beach. They often shared dinner, alternating at Garth's cottage and at theirs. Garth was so tender with Megan, so patient. When they were at his cottage, he provided her with reams of drawing paper, pencils and crayons and colored felt markers. He always took time to explain things to her and let her borrow the books he'd illustrated.

October soon turned into early November and there was a week of stormy weather. The coastal winter had begun. The restaurant was closed. The McDermotts were getting ready to leave for Mexico. They planned a big farewell party for the staff, encouraging each of them to bring a friend. Val debated whether or not to ask Garth. He knew the McDermotts and she knew he would be welcome. But she wasn't sure she wanted any speculation among The Seawinds group about their relationship. It was Eileen herself that settled the question for Val.

"Of course, you'll bring Megan." She pulled a sad face. "Tom and I are sure going to miss her. Our daughter and grandchildren are coming to us for Christmas, but Megan is special." It warmed Val's heart to know the McDermotts loved her little daughter. She started to ask Eileen about bringing Garth, but her employer surprised her by saying, "Why don't you ask Garth Hasten to come with you two? I know he's a kind of workaholic, but he probably gets lonely and would like a chance to get out and be with other people."

"Okay, I'll ask him," Val said, glad that the decision had been made for her.

Garth accepted at once. He seemed very pleased to have been asked.

At the prospect of the party, Val realized she hadn't been anywhere, done anything like that, in over a year. The idea of getting dressed up was strange and rather exciting. The only thing she wore other than jeans and a sweater was the maroon poplin jacket worn by the employees at the hardware store and her waitress uniform. On impulse, she bought herself a new dress. When she'd taken Megan over to Oceanview for a dental checkup, she'd spotted it in the window of a small shop. It was on sale. After she tried it on, it took little urging from the salesclerk to convince her to buy it. It was a simple, classic design, with long sleeves, round neck, gently flowing skirt. Uncluttered, the kind of dress she pre-ferred. Kevin had gone for more sophisticated styles, like slinky sheaths awash in sequins. Her hair had been fair for so many years that it had never occurred to her to choose something this shade, a deep apricot. But with her hair now its natural brown, the color was really becoming.

As she got dressed the night of the McDermotts' party, Val found herself humming. The dress fitted perfectly and the color was great, but it needed some jewelry to accent it. Val had sold most of the elaborate, expensive jewelry Kevin had given her over the years for much-needed cash. She'd kept only a few pieces that had sentimental value for her. She opened her dresser drawer and brought out her jewelry box. As she lifted it, she caught a glimpse of the blue legal folder underneath, and froze. She knew it contained the still-unsigned divorce papers. With one hand, she pushed the folder back farther out of sight. She wasn't going to think of that tonight, nor of Kevin, nor of any of the ugly past.

She opened the lid of the jewelry box and examined the contents. All that she had kept was a string of freshwater pearls, a coral necklace and a few pairs of earrings. She decided on the coral strand and small coral cluster studs. Then she saw the charm bracelet.

Kevin had given it to her in high school when they were the "in" thing. He'd had to pay for it in monthly installments out of the salary from his after-school job as a bagger in the local market. But it was fourteen-karat gold. Nothing cheap for Kevin.

She had loved it back then and each of the charms he had given her throughout their romance. The tiny pair of roller skates signifying their secret meetings at the skating rink, a tiny graduation cap marking her graduation two years after his, the tiny replica of engagement and wedding rings, the little cradle celebrating Megan's birth. All milestones in their life together. But after a while, Kevin didn't give her any more charms. He gave her other pieces, bigger, showier, more expensive.

Val replaced the bracelet, covered it with the velvet cushion that also hid the wide wedding ring she didn't wear any longer, closed the lid of the jewelry box and put it back in the drawer.

She studied herself in the mirror. She liked what she saw. It was much more "her" than she had ever seen before. The *real* her. The woman she really was, not the polished image Kevin had wanted her to be. For the first time in many years, she felt excited and happy.

Just then, Garth's signal knock sounded at the front door. Val heard the patter of Megan's feet in their brand-new patent leather shoes on the wooden floor as she ran to answer it, calling as she ran, "It's Garth, Mommy! Are you ready for the party?"

As ready as I'll ever be, Val said to the woman in the mirror. She grabbed her coat and went to greet Garth.

At The Seawinds, all was festive. Chef Johnny had outdone himself with a fabulous buffet, beautifully presented. Turkey, ham, salmon mousse, creamed potatoes, asparagus, five different kinds of salad, fruit compote, lemon cake, pecan pie. A selection of wines, pineapple punch, coffee. It was a lavish feast such as one he might have put on for a gala society affair in San Francisco. Several people had brought their children, too, so Megan had others to play with while the adults relaxed and thoroughly enjoyed themselves. Val realized what a friendly bunch her coworkers were and that she would miss them when the restaurant was closed. Garth seemed to fit right in as if he had been one of them and found it only natural to be there.

The McDermotts were looking forward to their restful time at their condo south of the border, but as the evening came to a close, Tom waxed a little nostalgic. He had everyone form a circle to sing "Auld Lang Syne," promising that they'd be back in March to open the restaurant and hoping that everyone would return to join them.

On the way home, Megan fell asleep in Garth's car and he carried her into the cottage and to her bedroom. She stirred sleepily as Val undressed her and tucked her in.

"Wasn't it fun, Mommy?" she asked drowsily. "The most fun we've had in a long time, wasn't it?" For some reason, the child's voice had a plaintive sound that went straight to Val's heart. Had she somehow infected her little girl with some of her own melancholy? Unintentionally, of course, but it had somehow been a shadow on their life. Then and there, Val promised herself that she was going to consciously try to change. Megan deserved more, deserved a mother who was optimistic, positive, and a childhood as happy and worry free as possible.

When Val went back out to the front room, Garth was standing at the window looking out at the sea. The frosty-looking moon was shining on the water, shedding a luminous light on the rippling waves.

"Come here, Val, this is too lovely to miss," he said without turning around. She went and stood beside him.

She felt his arm go around her shoulders and pull her close to him. She drew in her breath. She felt a shock of delight at his nearness and a strong, sweet emotion rose within her.

It had been so long since she'd been this close to a man. So close she could smell the tweedy scent of his jacket, feel the strength of his fingers tightening on her arm through the material of her dress. For a few seconds, she longed to let her head rest against his shoulder, let him hold her, comfort her. Comfort? She wasn't sure what she meant by that. She just knew it was wonderful and she wanted it to go on and on.

"Val, Val," he said softly, caressingly. He moved as if to turn her around and into his arms.

The tenderness in his voice alerted her and she stepped away, her heart hammering in her throat. Danger zone, something warned. Garth pulled her gently back to him, put his hand under her chin and lifted her face so she had to look at him.

"Val, I've been wanting to do this all evening," he said. "I've been wanting to do this for weeks."

He leaned down and kissed her, a kiss whose sweetness she wanted to savor and which she reluctantly ended.

"Val, I—" Garth started to say, but she placed her fingers on his lips, shook her head.

"No, Garth, please. Don't say anything."

"But why? I want to tell you how I feel—"

"Please don't. I don't want to hear it."

"Why not? Don't you know, haven't you guessed that I—"

"It's too soon, Garth."

"Too soon for what? To say that I care for you? That I know I can make you happy?"

She didn't answer, just shook her head.

"Or do you mean too soon since...after your husband?"

That seemed the simplest explanation. How else could she possibly explain that it would be fatal if she took what he was saying seriously, flung herself into his arms, into the safety and security of this good, dear man, and let him love her? She had lied to him. She was living a lie. And Garth was so honest, so open, so loving. It shouldn't have happened. She shouldn't have let it happen.

"Just try to understand, Garth. I can't say any more."

Garth sighed, frowned, then said, "All right, I won't press you, Val. But someday...someday soon, you'll have to let me say it and you'll have to listen."

He let go her hands and she walked with him to the door.

"Good night, Val," he said, and waited for some response.

"Good night, Garth. Thank you for everything."

After he left, Val pressed her hands against her flaming cheeks. She was trembling. It had been close. All her feelings for Garth, the feelings of which she had been vaguely aware had rushed to the surface tonight with his touch, with his kiss. Val closed her eyes, squeezing them tight, and from the corners tears rolled slowly out. It would have been so easy, so lovely, to give in, to let Garth take her in his arms, love her. No matter what she felt, this was not in her plan. Her life did not include sharing love. She had too many secrets. If Garth knew, he would despise her for not being honest. She had skated too close to the edge, she had to back off, before everyone would be hurt.

Chapter Fifteen

The days following the McDermotts' farewell party were filled with contradictory emotions for Val. What had happened between her and Garth disturbed her. It should never have happened. It was her fault. She had given in to the impulse of the moment. The longing for companionship, comfort.

She had been aware of her growing attraction to Garth Hasten. As their friendship had developed, she saw in him all the things she admired in a man—intelligence, consideration, sensitivity along with a strength that was masculine without being macho. He didn't seem to feel the need to prove anything. He was just himself. The more she had come to admire him, the more she was drawn to him.

Was it love? Perhaps, not yet. But she had to be honest. It could easily become love if she allowed it to happen. The trouble was that she wasn't free to love Garth or anyone else. Legally, she was still married. And she had lied to Garth about that. That troubled her most.

He had been so open with her and she had kept the deepest, most important thing about herself a secret.

Before she could let anything more develop between her and Garth, her marriage to Kevin must be dissolved. The divorce papers were still unsigned. Val felt the most wrenching indecision at the thought. How would Garth react when she told him the truth? Because that's what she had to do or…or what? Run away? Again? She was done with trying to escape from the past. She wanted a normal life for both Megan and herself.

After a third restless night, feeling groggy from lack of sleep, Val dragged herself out of bed. She went through the motions of fixing breakfast and walking with Megan to meet the school bus. Then she walked back down the beach and headed toward the cove. Her head ached from the inner confusion, the indecision that racked her brain and bruised her heart. Over and over she asked herself questions that seemed to have no answers. No right answers anyway. Were there any right answers?

Should she do what Kevin had demanded? Sign the papers, get it over with once and for all? If she did, then she would be free. Free. That word had a strange, unpredictable ring. She hadn't really been free since the first time she saw Kevin.

He'd been coming down the hall in high school, with his stocky, muscular body, a swagger in his walk, his head held in a defiant way. He'd stood in front of her and her friend, Ellen, on their way to class and boldly asked her, "Where do you hang out after school?"

Hang out? Even then, she could only imagine what her schoolteacher mother would say to that kind of talk! Why had she let Kevin take over her life? Was it the novelty of opposites attracting? Or rebellion against her sheltered environment, conservative parents? Had they been, as her mother had tried to point out to her, "unequally yoked" even from the beginning?

"It will never work," her father had said. "Oil and water. You're too different, come from too different backgrounds. You're a smart girl, Valerie, be sensible." Both parents had begged her to stay away from him. All their dire predictions had fallen on deaf ears. Val was infatuated. She hadn't listened. She'd gone headlong into disaster.

Disaster? The description startled Val. Had her marriage been a disaster? She tried to think back, to remember. Scenes flickered one after the other like slides in a projector of her mind. Incidents, events, parties, celebrations, arguments, excitement, birthdays, anniversaries, romantic occasions. Kevin elated, Kevin moody, Kevin angry… Theirs had been a turbulent relationship. But they had loved each other. Hadn't they?

Lost in her own confused thoughts, Val walked to the end of the inlet, then turned back and began going in the other direction. The ocean was sluggish, a pewter color. The sky, heavy with gray clouds, matched her dreary mood. She walked along, head down. Today Megan was going home with Bonnie after kindergarten, so there was no need to hurry home. Val trudged on, not knowing how long she'd been on the beach. Then, suddenly, she found herself at the foot of the narrow wooden steps that led to Garth's cottage. She stopped and looked up toward the small weathered house.

Even as she did, his door opened and he came bounding down the steps toward her, calling her name as he ran. As he approached her, he was smiling. "I've been thinking about you all morning," he said. "I was trying to decide whether to come and get you, snatch you away from whatever you were doing." Then as if he saw something in her expression that troubled him, his smile faded. He put both hands on her shoulders and looked deep into her eyes. For a full moment, they simply stood there not saying anything. "Is something wrong?" he asked.

How could she tell him it was their relationship, her growing feelings for him that were troubling her? That lately she had become aware of how much she looked forward to their times togcthcr. After all she'd been through, she'd wondered if she would ever be able to feel again, even to love, but getting to know Garth had answered that question. Val realized that a man like Garth was someone she could trust and love. There was something special about him that gave her the hope that the kind of relationship she had always longed for but wasn't sure was possible could indeed exist. Now that realization frightened her.

"I just made a pot of coffee. Come on," Garth said, taking hold of her hand and pulling on it gently.

Val hesitated for just one moment, then wordlessly she went with him over the dunes, up the steps of the cottage.

Inside, the fire in the stove crackled. Garth helped her off with her jacket. He poured coffee for both of them and placed the mugs on the table. "I want to show you some new sketches," he told her. "My idea for a new book. They're rough, but I want your opinion. As you'll see, I used some of Megan. I did it—" he grinned "—without your permission, I'm afraid. I did them one afternoon when we were at the cove. Later, when I was looking at them—well, it all just came together. With the right words, they could be made into a picture book that would teach kids about shells and tide pools. Anyway, I'd like to see what you think."

He brought his sketchbook over to the table and Val began slowly turning the pages. Garth was certainly a skilled artist. Even though he had identified them as rough, the drawings were exceptionally good and he had caught Megan perfectly. Val's eyes misted slightly as she saw how he had captured the movements of her tiny body, her delicate profile as she bent over a tide pool, examined a shell.

"These are wonderful," she said finally.

"I haven't submitted them to my agent yet, obviously. I want to do a couple of finished paintings, then present the proposal." He added almost shyly, "I hoped you'd like them."

"I do."

They spent more time discussing the layout of the proposed book, Val contributing some ideas that Garth enthusiastically agreed he could incorporate in the text. He refilled their coffee mugs several times and neither was aware of the passage of time. Finally, Garth closed the sketchbook and pushed it aside. "Thank you. Your suggestions were great. I should give you credit as my collaborator when it's published." Impulsively, he leaned over and kissed her lightly.

Somewhere far away, she could hear the pounding of the surf and yet it all seemed unreal. Nothing seemed real. Then reality broke through. Startled, Val drew back.

"I have to go. I shouldn't have come."

"Don't say that, Val. Don't spoil it," Garth protested. "I tried to tell you before that I feel we were somehow meant to be together. Why else would our paths have crossed for the second time?"

"I don't know. I never meant for this to happen."

"Neither did I. But it did. We can't deny what we feel." He caught her hand. "I care a great deal about you, Val."

"Don't say that," Val said sharply. She pulled her hand away and stood up.

"But it's the truth," Garth protested.

Val walked into the middle of the room. Her back to him she said, "Please, don't tell me that. You don't know me—you don't know anything about me...

"I have to go." She whirled around, eyes wide, desperate. "Where's my jacket?"

Garth went over to her. "Okay, okay," he said gently. "Everything's all right. I didn't mean to rush you. We'll take our time. Get to know each other longer, if that's what you want. If that's what it takes. Can't I hope? Can't you let yourself care for me?"

"You're far too nice, Garth." She shook her head. "I don't deserve it." Tears started rolling down her cheeks.

"You deserve a great deal more," he said very softly. He leaned to her and wiped away the tears with his thumbs. "Please don't cry. I want to make you happy."

She looked up at him, wondering if it was possible to be happy? Could she allow herself to be happy? She glanced at her watch. "Oh, no, I have to go. Mrs. Faraday will be bringing Mcgan back. I have to get up to Mitchell's service station to meet her."

"Let me drive you," Garth offered.

"No, I need to walk. Get out in the fresh air. Clear my brain," Val said. "I feel all mixed up."

Garth held her face in his hands a moment longer, gazing down at her.

"I really do have to go, Garth," Val repeated, fighting the urge to stay with him.

He laughed softly, then held her a little longer, reciting the old nursery rhyme, "'Ladybug, ladybug, fly away home. Your house is on fire and your children alone.'" Then he released her. "Okay, I'll let you go for now."

Out in the wind, Val ran along the ocean where the tide had left the sand hard, then scrambled up the dunes to Beach Road. She was out of breath from running when she saw Mrs. Faraday's station wagon come in sight.

Val thanked Bonnie's mother and waved as they drove away. Taking Megan's hand, she started back down the beach to their cottage. Megan chattered about her day with her friends, then looked up at Val and asked, "So what did you do all day, Mommy?"

Immediately, Val felt a rush of guilt. She thought of the hamper of clothes she had meant to take to the Laundromat, the list of groceries she should have brought with her. To say she had been with Garth most of the day would only bring more questions. Again she thought of what had happened between them.

She looked down at Megan's little face. And she saw Kevin's deep blue eyes. They were expecting an answer. In that moment, Val was struck by her features. Undeniable. The eyes, the shape of her nose—Megan was Kevin's child and Val was still legally married to her father. No matter what she felt for Garth Hasten, before their relationship went any further, she had to end her marriage to Kevin. Val felt a painful twinge. That was the real question. Was she ready to end her marriage—free herself forever?

Chapter Sixteen

All the next day, Val's thoughts were in conflict. She had to admit her feelings for Garth were strong. But she also realized she wasn't free to indulge them. Not free because of her own indecision. Not free because she hadn't used the key she'd been given to unlock her own imprisoned heart.

Things were still unresolved the next morning. She was dressed for work and in the kitchen making coffee when a tap came on the door. It was Garth. She opened it wider for him to come in, but he shook his head. "No, Val, I just stopped by to tell you. I wanted you to know that I have no intention of pressuring you or pushing our relationship any further than you're ready to go." He looked at her intently. "I care very much about you. And Megan. I don't want anything to ruin what we already have. You'll set the limits. That's what I wanted you to know. I want to be your friend. More than that, if you want it, too. But only then."

"Thank you, Garth," Val murmured. She felt almost overwhelmed by such honesty, his generosity of heart.

He smiled then. "Just so it's understood. I don't want to lose you, okay?"

"Okay." She smiled in return.

After he left, Val knew she had to tell Garth her real situation, tell him the truth about Kevin, that he wasn't dead but in prison. It wasn't fair to let him go on thinking…what? That she was available? She would just have to find the right time. It wasn't something you just blurted out.

Good intentions are one thing; carrying them out another thing entirely. Days passed. The opportunity never seemed to present itself, the time wasn't ever quite right. Garth was now finishing up a project, several illustrations for a book with a January deadline looming. With Val's work hours, her regular everyday life as a single mom, their time together was limited.

A stormy Pacific-coast November ushered in a surprisingly mild December. Mornings were sunny and often the afternoons were too, although short. On such days, they managed to take long walks on the beach, usually accompanied by Megan, who had formed a strong attachment to Garth. Val noticed this with both pleasure and pain. It was the kind of relationship she had wanted Megan to have with Kevin.

That had never happened. Kevin had never spent the time with his child that Garth seemed to enjoy. Kevin was too impatient, and especially after they learned about Megan's deafness, he'd seemed to lose interest. That seemed a harsh judgment on a child's father. Sad as it was, Val had to admit it was true. Sometimes watching the tall man and the little girl, their heads bent together examining a tide pool or walking along swinging hands, Val had a fleeting dream wish—that this caring, special guy was Megan's father, the kind of father the little girl deserved. Val knew it was probably wrong of her to think such thoughts. Still, the contrast between Garth's relationship with Megan and Kevin's was too glaring not to notice.

Before school closed for the holidays, Megan's teacher sent home a note with her inviting them to the Christmas program to be held at her church in Oceanview. She wrote, "The Sunday-school children will have their own performance, and from what my sister tells me, it should have special interest to you and Megan."

"Would you like to go?" Val asked Megan after reading the note.

"Oh, yes, Mommy."

Arrangements were made for them to meet Miss Pierson outside the church and sit with her and her family. When Garth heard about the plan, he insisted on driving them. "It'll be a long bus ride and probably cold," he insisted firmly, cutting off any argument on Val's part.

As they pulled up outside the church, Val impulsively asked, "Would you like to come in with us?"

There was a moment's hesitation, then Garth asked, "Do you think it would be all right?"

"I don't see why not."

"Okay, I'd like to." He circled the parking lot for a space and pulled in. Val noticed he had on a shirt and tie. Maybe he had hoped he'd be invited to come along with them. She was glad she had. From the looks of the assembled congregation, it was a family sort of activity. Miss Pierson, waiting just inside the door, greeted them and was introduced.

The church was festively decorated with swags of evergreens. Bunches of crimson-berried holly hung over all the tall, narrow windows. Clusters of red bows were tied at the end of each pew. A tree trimmed with gold stars, strings of glittering beads and topped with a gilt angel, stood majestically at the side of the altar.

Sitting beside Garth in the darkened church, lit by dozens of red candles, Val felt a wonderful warmth she had never before experienced. Kevin had never gone to church with her. Not that it was an excuse or a reason, but little by little in the years of their marriage, she had given up going herself. She glanced at Garth, then at Megan, and she had a sense of completion, a rightness about the three of them here together in God's house.

She did not have a chance to delve very deeply into her feelings because the program was beginning. There was a rustling, a shuffling of feet, the murmur of children's voices, followed by adult sounds of "Shhh." Then the piano struck the first notes of a familiar Christmas carol and two lines of little boys and girls from five years of age to about seven or eight, marched down the aisle and took their places in double rows at the front of the church. The girls wore red dresses of various styles, the boys white shirts with red bow ties. A young woman, evidently their Sunday-school teacher, stood facing them.

With a nod from her, the children all took big breaths and began to sing. "Away in a manger, no crib for His bed, the Little Lord Jesus…" The high, sweet, piping voices, a little off-key, rang out. But it was the other thing they were doing that caught Val's attention. They were signing, their small hands forming the beautiful gestures of the language of the deaf. Val drew in her breath. She felt Garth's hand take hers and squeeze it. Val looked down at Megan, who was watching spellbound.

When the carol was over, the teacher turned to the congregation and asked, "Would you like to sing the next hymn along with us? It's one I'm sure you all know and the signs are very simple. I'll go through it once or twice, then we can all sing it together."

The pianist played the tune through one time as the teacher demonstrated how to sign the words, "Jesus loves me, this I know, 'cause the Bible tells me so."

Val heard Garth's deep baritone rise along with her higher voice. "Yes, Jesus loves me. Yes, Jesus loves me." He was joining right in as if he had been doing it all his life. She would have to ask him sometime about his church background. They had never spoken about spiritual things…. She felt there was much more to learn about this man.

From Garth, Val turned to look at Megan and saw to her delight that Megan was signing along with everyone else and seemed to be thoroughly enjoying herself.

Everyone was invited to the parish hall for coffee, punch and cake after the service. Miss Pierson came up to them. "How did you like the program?" she asked Val hopefully. While they chatted, Garth wandered away hand in hand with Megan. Out of the corner of her eye, Val saw them in conversation with two ladies, one she recognized as the pianist. What on earth were they talking about? And how did Garth explain his presence here with Megan? Curious, Val asked Megan about it after they'd gone home and she was helping her get ready for bed.

"What were you and Garth talking to those ladies about?"

Megan dimpled and said, "They thought he was my daddy."

Val felt a small, anxious twinge. "So what did you tell them?"

"I didn't tell them anything. Garth did." Megan gave a little bounce on her bed before getting under the sheets.

"And what did he say?"

"He said he was a friend of the family!" Megan laughed. "Wasn't that funny, Mommy? A friend of the family!"

"Well, he is, isn't he?" Val said rather breathlessly as she tucked Megan in.

"He's more than that, Mommy." Megan frowned.

Again Val felt a little twinge. How much had Megan noticed? What did she think about Garth?

"Oh?"

"You know. He's our neighbor."

Slightly relieved, Val kissed her daughter good-night and put out the lamp. Once more, she felt guilty for not leveling with Garth about Kevin. Sooner or later, she had to do it. Then and only then, could she make some decision about her next step.

That night, she got out the blue legal folder and read over the divorce papers. To sign and file them, she would have to return them to Brad Hensley, and he in turn would have to notify Kevin.

With the holidays coming, it somehow seemed the worst time to do this. Christmas must be the bleakest time of year for all prison inmates. She shoved the folder back in the drawer again. She couldn't do that to Kevin. Pour salt on the open wound of his despair.

Kevin had always made a big deal about Christmas. Not the religious part but the decorations, the presents, the glitz. They always had to have the most lights in the yard, the showiest wreath on the front door, the tallest tree in the neighborhood, sparkling with ornaments and shimmering tinsel. Every year they gave a party right before the twenty-fifth so that people could see the piles of gaudily wrapped gifts under the tree. It used to embarrass Val when she heard Kevin boast to some of their guests about the presents he was giving her. It was always something splashy, extravagant, something she didn't need or even want.

Poor Kevin. What would his Christmas this year be like? In spite of what he'd said, Val thought she'd send a small package to him, things the prison wouldn't prohibit. Some of that Danish chocolate he liked… How could Kevin object to that?

This Christmas would be nothing like their Christmases in Meadowbrook. However, Eileen had told Val earlier that she and Tom wanted to give Megan one of the dolls from the "Americana Collection." "I'm a doll collector myself. And these are so special," Eileen laughingly confessed to Val. "Since I don't have a granddaughter of my own to give one to, indulge me, please." Of course, Val and Megan had both seen those dolls, but the price tag was way too much for Val to consider. When Val protested, Eileen had quickly contradicted, "Now, Val, we insist. We want to do it. In fact, I've already ordered it out of the catalog. Just think how happy she'll be on Christmas morning."

Val knew Megan would be overjoyed. So she had gratefully agreed to the gift. She had put away a few other small things for Megan, as well. There would be a doll bed and a set of tiny dishes, a new dress. They would have a table tree with homemade decorations, string dried cranberries and popcorn, and make a star out of aluminum foil.

It was Garth who came up with the most wonderful holiday plan. "I want to take you and Megan up to San Francisco for the annual production of *The Nutcracker*. I was thinking of a matinee, on a Saturday or Sunday. We'll have lunch at some fancy place and see the store windows and decorations and have one heck of a time. How does that sound?"

"It sounds fabulous!" Val exclaimed. "I know Megan will love it." Val was deeply touched at his having suggested something like this that they could share together with Megan. "Thank you, Garth."

It was a special day. San Francisco at Christmastime was a magical place. The streets were beautifully decorated; store windows had creative displays, scenes from favorite Christmas stories, with life-size puppets representing characters out of Dickens or some other famous holiday tale. The sound of carols filled the air as the revolving doors opened, sending the familiar melodies out into the street. Valiant Salvation Army workers rang their bells, shoppers thronged the sidewalks with their bulging shopping bags from which rolls of bright wrapping paper emerged. There was a marvelous Santa Claus to be visited and Megan got to sit on his lap and whisper what she wanted. Her eyes were shining as she rejoined Val with the candy cane he had given her. She skipped between them, holding on to both their hands as they walked toward the restaurant where they planned to have lunch before going to the theater.

The Nutcracker was fantastic, with its wonderful costumes, music and dancing. Megan was totally enthralled. She sat on the edge of her seat between Val and Garth, her face reflecting her absolute joy. She hardly moved throughout the entire performance.

Driving back to Seawood through the dark night, the little girl was quiet, still wrapped up in the enchantment of the ballet. When they got home and Val was putting her to bed, Megan said dreamily, "I wish I could have a dream like Clara's, Mommy."

"You can have your own dream, sweetie."

"Today was sort of like a dream, wasn't it?" Megan said as she climbed under the covers.

"Yes, darling, it was." Val kissed the flushed cheeks.

And it had been. Val couldn't remember being as happy for a whole day as she had been today. Almost guiltily, she remembered she hadn't thought of Kevin once. It had seemed so perfect, so complete, just the three of them.

Garth was heating them some cranberry juice in a saucepan on the woodstove when Val came out of Megan's room.

"All settled?"

"Yes, and she's one happy little girl. Oh, Garth, how

can I thank you? Megan had such a wonderful day. One I know she'll never forget."

"It was wonderful for me, too, Val." He stopped stirring, ladled out a cup of the steaming beverage and handed it to her. She took it and sat down in one of the wicker chairs. He stood looking at her before taking a seat in the chair opposite. "I felt like a family," he said, then added, "Did you?"

Over the rim of the cup, Val met his gaze. Was this the time to tell him? Tell him that, yes, it had felt that way to her, too? But she didn't have the right to feel that way.

"Don't answer that," he said before she could get her thoughts together. "It was an unfair question." He paused. "So, let's talk about Christmas. I'm going to have to go to New York the week after, but we can have a good, old-fashioned Christmas." He launched into some ideas and plans.

Not wanting to spoil his enthusiasm as he outlined his plans, Val let the moment she might have told him about Kevin slip by.

Garth insisted on bringing the turkey for their Christmas dinner. Because neither of their cottages had an adequate stove to do the job, he decided to have it roasted at a bakery in Oceanview that specialized in holiday catering. Val was to furnish the vegetables and salad. Of course, when Garth showed up on Christmas morning, he brought much more than the bird. Val looked on in mock astonishment as he unloaded bag after bag, all kinds of fruit, oranges, apples, a pineapple, bananas, candy and ice cream and a bottle of sparkling cider. He also had several gaily wrapped packages for Megan.

"Oh, Garth, you're a regular Santa Claus. You're making a believer out of me." Val laughed, delighted but somewhat taken aback. She had only a small gift for him, a desk calendar, and Megan had made him a pencil holder at school out of papier-mâché and painted it herself. "You really are too kind," Val said as they looked over at Megan, who was happily playing with her new doll, pretending to read to her from the big, beautiful book Garth had given her.

"Not kind at all. I get a great deal of pleasure doing things for you and Megan." He reached over and took Val's hand. "Don't you realize that, Val?"

For a minute, Garth's gaze held hers as if searching for some answer he desperately wanted to hear.

She hesitated and almost spoke, but he quickly dropped her hand, got up and went behind the kitchen divider, saying, "Let's open the cider. It's a celebration, isn't it?" He worked at the cork.

"I guess so," Val said.

"Not sure? Well, come over here and I'll tell you." He poured out the bubbly liquid into glasses he'd brought and held one out to her.

"What are we celebrating, besides Christmas?"

"Do we really have to have more of a reason other than we've found each other?" Garth asked in a low voice.

Involuntarily, Val looked over her shoulder at Megan. But she was completely engaged in the tea party she was having with her doll.

"I don't care if Megan knows how I feel about you,"

Garth said, raising his glass in a toasting gesture. "I'd like the whole world to know it."

"Garth, there's something—" Val started to say, but Garth shook his head and put down his glass on the counter.

"I almost forgot," he said. "I've got a little present for you."

"But you've done so much already...the turkey and all the fixings and Megan's gifts."

"This is a special one. Just for you." He reached into his jacket pocket and brought out a small square box. It was wrapped in shiny gold paper and had a gauzy silk bow. It looked like the size jewelry might come in. Val took it warily.

"Go on, open it," Garth directed.

Val untied the ribbon with trembling hands and lifted out a gray suede box. When she opened it, she met Garth's smiling eyes and couldn't help smiling, too. It was a gold pin in the shape of a ladybug, sparkling with tiny red stones outlining its distinctive markings.

"Remember, 'Ladybug, ladybug, fly away home'?" he asked gently.

How could she forget the day she'd run home, her heart pounding, escaping what she was feeling. Fled for her life, actually.

"Yes, I remember," Val replied. They looked at each other for a long moment. In that look was all that was unspoken but could no longer be denied.

The undercurrent of excitement between them permeated the rest of the day. Everything seemed to glow. With each glance, each casual word or touch, the heightened feeling increased. As they talked, joked, everything seemed touched with a kind of magic. They were more loving toward Megan. They played checkers and did a puzzle with her and laughed easily over everything.

At last it was time for Megan to go to bed.

When it was time to say her prayers, Megan jolted Val by asking, "Do you think Harriet gave Flynn an extra big bone for his Christmas dinner?" Val was startled. Megan had not mentioned their dog or Harriet or their life before Seawood in a long time. That didn't mean the child hadn't thought about them, of course. Did she also think of Kevin?

That idea sent a chill through Val, taking some of the shining happiness of this day from her. As she groped for something reassuring to say in response to Megan's question, Val was acutely conscious that Garth was waiting for her in the other room. But suddenly the shadow of Kevin was there, intruding in whatever future they might have.

"Sweet dreams, sweetheart." Val kissed Megan, turned on the night-light and went to the door. Her hand on the knob, she hesitated. She knew Garth was waiting, waiting for this moment when they would be alone. Her heart quickened. She had to head off whatever he had hoped for, what she herself longed to do. She opened the door and went out into the front room. Ignoring the eager look on his face, she went straight past him to the stove. There she stood holding out her suddenly cold hands to its warmth. Behind her she heard his footsteps, next she felt his arms go around her waist. Immediately she moved away, "No, no—"

"Why not, Val? We can't deny our feelings for each other any longer."

Val closed her eyes, held her breath, desperately trying to recall the words of Scripture that she had tried to memorize. "God is faithful, Who will not allow you to be tempted beyond what you are able." But they seemed hollow in the face of the great temptation of the moment, the need, the longing for love and safety she knew she could experience with Garth.

She felt his hands on her shoulders, his breath in her ear, as he whispered, "Don't be afraid, darling. I love you...."

She felt a sob rise in her throat. With tremendous effort, she broke away, shaking and breathless. More real than ever, she felt Kevin's shadow—tortured, trapped, hovering. She could feel the shackles of the love that still bound her, ones from which she could not break free. It was no use. No matter how she tried to block out his image, it was impossible.

"What is it, Val? What's wrong? Did I do something? Say something? Answer me."

She shuddered, then slowly turned toward him. His expression was puzzled. Indecision gripped her. Was this the time to tell Garth that her husband, who instead of being dead as she pretended, was alive? That she had lied? In that split second, Val knew it was too late; her lie was now forcing her into another. To deny that she loved Garth. She had dug her own pit from which she couldn't see any escape.

Garth gave a deep sigh. "Well, I guess I misread the signals again. I wanted a commitment from you. I love you so much...." There was discouragement and defeat in his voice. "You're not ready to break with the past, are you, Val? That's it, isn't it?"

She couldn't answer. She felt too ashamed at what she had done. Lied, let him care, let him hope that something was possible between them. She forced herself to look at Garth. Saw naked pain in his eyes, the reflection of his wounded heart. Should she try to explain that it wasn't his fault, nothing he had said or done? It was because she couldn't free herself from a love that kept her prisoner.

Val put out her hand to touch his arm, but Garth had already moved away. He stood, picked up his sport jacket, slung it over one shoulder, then turned to face her.

"Well, I can't compete with a dead man," he said tightly. Then, without another word, he walked to the door. His hand on the doorknob, he turned back. "Goodbye, Val." Then he was gone.

The bang of the door resounded in the silent cottage. The echo of that door's slam would ring in Val's ears for a long time.

Chapter Seventeen

The New Year Val had looked forward to was ushered in by a fierce Pacific storm. Rain rattled the windows of their cottage, wind howled around the corners, penetrated the thin walls. The ocean looked dark, angry, as turbulent as Val's emotions.

Christmas had come and gone and she had not heard from Garth. A hundred times the accusation he had flung at her had resounded in her mind. "You're not ready to break with the past, are you, Val?" The sound of the door banging behind him echoed in her aching heart just like his parting shot. "Well, I can't compete with a dead man."

Every morning since, Val had looked out her window down the beach to Garth's cottage. But there was no spiral of smoke from the chimney, no lights at night. She walked along Beach Road to check, saw that his carport was empty, the car gone.

She felt crushed. She hadn't realized how much Garth had come to mean to her. Maybe it had taken this. Garth had left Seawood without even telling her, without even saying goodbye, without her having told him the truth.

The weeks that followed passed slowly, filled with regrets, longings and the vague hope that Garth would relent, that he would come back, that somehow things could be straightened out between them. Even after she had told him, would he ever forgive her for lying to him all these months?

Maybe it wasn't meant to be after all. Maybe their lives had been too different. Maybe she came with too much baggage for any relationship. Maybe Garth was right. Maybe she couldn't break with the past. Maybe it was just her and Megan against the world that Kevin had thrust them into. Maybe she shouldn't dream of the possibilities of anything else. Just play the hand she'd been dealt.

The fact that she'd brought this second heartbreak on herself didn't help. Much as she tried, the oppressive loneliness descended again. Megan was vocal about missing Garth. She asked about him constantly. But Val had no answer for her persistent "When is Garth coming home?"

January dragged into February and two important things happened that directed Val's attention from her own heartache. Megan brought a note home from the school nurse saying that during a routine hearing check, it was noted that Megan's hearing loss was acute. She recommended that Megan see a specialist. Of course, this was no shock to Val. She had been warned that the hearing loss was progressive. Megan had adapted so well and compensated in so many ways for her deafness that Val realized she had, too.

Now the question was, should she take her to San Francisco to see the doctor they had consulted before? She felt sure he would only repeat his diagnosis, make the same suggestions to prepare Megan for total hearing loss that he had before. She decided to talk to Miss Pierson, Megan's teacher before making any further decisions. She made an appointment to see her.

The teacher was sympathetic. "Megan is so bright and is always so attentive, especially at story time, it would be hard for anyone who didn't know her to tell she's hearing impaired." She went on, "I did talk to my sister during Christmas vacation. She said it would be a good idea to start teaching her to sign. But since she already has language and understands, it would be a natural progression to help her practice reading lips. Both skills for someone like Megan would be valuable." Before Val left, Miss Pierson suggested, "I wish you and Megan would come to our church some Sunday. As you know from the Christmas program, we have a wonderful lady who signs when the choir is singing. It's really lovely. I think you'd enjoy it. And it might be a way to start Megan on signing, to learn hymns."

Val thanked her and thought the suggestion a good one. The very next Sunday, she and Megan took the bus to Oceanside to Miss Pierson's church. As the teacher had told them, the signing of the choir's hymn selections was beautiful. After the service, Miss Pierson waited for them and introduced them to the choir leader who signed. She gave Val a small booklet with pictures of the hand movements for signing so that they could practice at home.

This proved a special shared experience for Megan

and Val. Each evening at supper and bedtime, they signed to each other. They made a game of learning together. It seemed to bring them even closer.

The worst time for Val was when Megan was asleep. That's when the little cottage seemed vast and empty. Curled up in front of the stove, bundled in a thick sweater, she tried to study her speed-writing and business math. But it was hard to concentrate since her mind kept wandering. The eerie sound of the wind didn't help and the fog that sometimes enveloped the house made her feel cut off from the world. Alone. Hard as she fought the depression, it seemed to creep over her like a smothering blanket.

The second thing that happened, unlike the progress of Megan's deafness, was totally unexpected. She received a letter from the prison chaplain. It was a shock. She had heard nothing since her disastrous visit in the summer. As she opened it, she was a little apprehensive, thinking he might have been angry that she'd rejected his advice about not visiting until Kevin asked to see her. The chaplain's letter was brief.

He merely stated that Kevin had sat in on a couple of his group sessions. He felt this was an indication that Kevin might eventually accept counseling. Even if it didn't, the chaplain observed that Kevin's general attitude was less hostile, less withdrawn. He didn't mention whether Kevin had said anything about the Christmas box she'd sent. Of course, she'd heard nothing.

The news from the prison chaplain brought a mixed reaction. One was that it brought the past rushing back. All the things Val had deliberately tried not to think about, tried to forget.

She sat holding the letter for a long time. Kevin was not dead as Garth believed. He existed. He was a living, breathing human being, no matter what, no matter that he never wrote, never communicated. The second reaction Val had was that it didn't really matter anymore. The truth was that not hearing from Kevin didn't hurt as much as not hearing from Garth. Val was glad when the McDermotts returned from Mexico in March and preparations began for the reopening of the restaurant. She was happy to see them and they were eager to see Megan and hear about her winter. They had brought presents for Megan—some maracas, gaily painted wooden gourds—and a beautiful embroidered blouse and a pair of dangly silver earrings for her.

"We missed you two," Eileen told Val, hugging her. When Val told them about taking the business course, Eileen suggested she could work part-time in the office. "I could use some help. It would be great if you could do some of the filing, correspondence and billing."

It seemed a wonderful opportunity to hone her new skills. It meant adjusting her hours, dividing the office work from her waitressing shift and making additional arrangements for Megan. But the extra money was helpful. Val squirreled some of it away in a special savings account. It appeared certain that later on Megan would need some specialized training or to attend a private school.

The season was under way and again Val's life took on a pattern—work at The Seawinds in the restaurant and then in the office. She felt that at last she was gaining some confidence in her own abilities, not only to cope but to exercise some control over her circumstances.

Then one night, after Megan was asleep, there was a familiar knock on her door. At first, Val thought she was mistaken, that she imagined she'd heard it. Then it came again, and she jumped up from the table where she'd been studying and hurried to the door. There stood Garth.

"Garth!" She could hardly manage his name.

"Hello, Val." His voice was husky.

"When did you arrive? I didn't know—"

"I just got here. I drove down from the city. I've only been back in California a few days. I couldn't wait any longer. I had to come. Had to see you." He paused. "May I come in?"

"Of course." She opened the door wider and he stepped inside.

"I'm so glad to see you, Val. I passed your cottage on the way to mine but didn't see any lights. I was afraid… thought you might have moved—"

"No, I'm still here. We're still here. The Seawinds is open. I'm working there again." Her words were tumbling over each other. She was excited, happy, scared. Her heart was thudding.

"Val, there's so much I want to say, but first, I have to ask…" He paused. "Forgive me?"

"For what? There's nothing to forgive."

"Yes, there is. I was insensitive. I tried to push things. I should have understood. Given you more time before… well, I know that now. I hope it's not too late. I left angry, hurt. I guess I wanted it so much—wanted you and Megan in my life, wanted to have it all. I thought it was what you wanted, too, but…" He hesitated. "What I'm trying to say is this, Val, I want things to be on your terms. Okay? You name them. I'll go along with them. If friendship is all it will ever be, I'll live with that. I don't want to lose you. Give us another chance?"

The tears that sprang to Val's eyes blurred Garth's anxious face. She was too moved emotionally by all that he was offering to speak. All she could do was nod.

Everything changed after Garth came back into Val's life. She had learned the truth that you never know how much you value something until it is lost. Garth's return was like the sun breaking through heavy clouds. He brought warmth and laughter, his own zest for life, flowing back into theirs. Megan was overjoyed.

It was a wonderful spring and summer. They spent part of each day together; hours at the cove where Megan would play happily while Garth sketched and Val sunbathed. Sometimes they cooked Garth's catch over a fire, sheltered by the dunes. Garth taught Megan how to make s'mores—toasted marshmallows squashed between chocolate grahams—and they became the dessert of choice at the beach. They sang old camp songs from both Garth's and Val's childhood. Afterward, Megan would curl up on a blanket and go to sleep while Val and Garth sat watching the driftwood fire.

Other times, they alternated supper at his cottage or theirs. Megan was a part of everything they did. Garth began to learn sign language and made it even more of a fun game. He was always thinking up things for them to do together. He was so thoughtful of her, suggested taking her to the carnival at Dorado Beach and watching the big fireworks display at Harbor Beach on the Fourth of July.

For Val, it was an inevitable comparison of what kind of father Kevin had been with the possibility of what kind of father Garth might prove to be.

Val was so happy that summer that she ignored the underlying problem beneath their growing closeness. Garth's quiet strength, his stable character, his always knowing what he wanted to be and achieving it—was also in marked contrast to Kevin's.

Although the word "marriage" was never actually spoken, it was always there between them. Val knew Garth was impatient for their friendship to grow into something more, but true to his word, he remained patient and accepted Val's unspoken terms.

Suddenly, she knew that she was in love with Garth, passionately in love with him. That the one thing in the world that would make her happier than she ever dreamed of being would be to marry him. He was everything she wanted, a man she could admire, trust and deeply love.

Now she realized that she had to tell Garth about her marriage. And, the time had come to make a decision about signing the divorce papers. She had avoided the problem long enough—too long perhaps. But now that she knew that she loved Garth, that their relationship was so much more than mere companionship, Val also knew she had a responsibility to him, and to all involved. Including Kevin.

Kevin. The thought of Kevin came back often. At the end of a wonderful day when she'd fallen asleep at night, Val would sometimes wake up with a start wondering about Kevin. He was still her husband.

From the distance of nearly two years, Val could now view their relationship, their marriage, with different eyes. Now she realized she had married a boy who had never grown up, a seriously flawed man. She had heard the attorney and the judge in court describe him as a person of poor moral judgment who was incapable of discerning right from wrong, who had rationalized his crime as poor timing rather than wrongdoing. He had taken a calculated risk and lost. If the odds had been different, he'd told Val, everything would have worked out. He hadn't seemed to realize even when she'd visited him in the county jail before the trial, that embezzling funds was a criminal act. Like everything else that had ever gone wrong in his life, he wasn't to blame.

She had been purposely blind to his faults. Why? Had she just married too young? Was she afraid to admit she had made a mistake, been stubbornly determined to make a bad marriage work? A kind of old-fashioned "you've made your bed, now lie in it" sort of mentality? But she didn't know any different. Hadn't really known any other man. Until now. Meeting Garth had changed her viewpoint of what a relationship could be.

Now she knew what she needed, what Megan needed, what neither of them had ever received in full measure from Kevin because he simply couldn't give it.

So what was keeping her from legally ending the marriage? Why were the divorce papers still unsigned?

It often kept Val sleepless knowing she should have told Garth about Kevin right from the beginning. And she certainly should have told him when he first came back to Seawood. Why did she keep putting it off? The answer was she feared Garth's reaction when he learned that she had lied to him. He would lose all respect for her, all trust in her. And though Val knew she'd deserve to lose his good opinion, she also knew how much her confession could hurt him, and she recoiled at the idea of hurting him.

The long days of summer moved on and still Val vacillated. Everything was so perfect. But as August drew to a close, Val knew she couldn't wait any longer.

Chapter Eighteen

The very next afternoon before she went to work, Val got out the blue legal folder that contained the divorce papers. Her feeling of guilt at not telling Garth the truth weighed heavily on her conscience.

She winced, remembering the reaction of one of their best friends in Meadowbrook, Dave Moore. After the news broke, she had come face-to-face with him at the shopping center. She would never forget his expression when he saw her. His eyes had narrowed, his face had twisted, and he'd almost spit out the words, "Don't tell me you didn't know what Kevin was up to. Any wife was bound to know. In my mind, you're every bit as guilty as he is."

Val was sure Dave was not the only one who felt the same. She was branded with Kevin's guilt. Would Garth find it just as hard to believe? Would he also doubt that it was possible to live with a man and not know him at all? She had only seen the shadow of the man, not the real person Kevin was. If she had...

The old panic rose within her again. Would she never

be free of it? Would it always be there somewhere, lurking like a coiled snake ready to lunge at her?

Yes, she knew she should have leveled with Garth right away. But how was she to know what they would become to each other? And how do you say to someone you've just met, "Oh, by the way, my husband is serving seven to fifteen years in the state penitentiary for embezzlement." That's some conversation starter, a real icebreaker. Val shuddered. She couldn't go back, undo anything. What she did now was the important thing.

She opened the folder, and on the top of the first page she read the title, Petition For The Dissolution Of Marriage. She turned the pages, skimming the legal terms she did not understand, moving along until the words began to dance and waver. Impatiently, she wiped away the unwanted tears. It was all so cold. Another legal document swam into her mind, one that had the same two names on it but instead read, Certificate Of Marriage.

It seemed to have nothing to do with her, the starry-eyed bride she had been at eighteen, standing beside Kevin in the tacky wedding chapel in Las Vegas. Nonetheless, he had bought her an orchid corsage and she had meant every word of the vows she repeated in a young, breathless voice. "I, Valerie take you, Kevin, to have and to hold from this day forward, for better for worse, for richer for poorer, in sickness and in health, to love and to cherish, till death…" Death. That's what she had promised. "Till death" not "dissolution."

Val sat down, holding the folder in suddenly trembling hands. She had wanted a good marriage. Given everything to make it so, tried to make Kevin happy.

She never dreamed that anything would happen to make it impossible for her to keep those vows.

She wasn't sure how long she sat there, wrapped in the past, incident after incident, memory after memory, floating into her mind. All at once, she glanced at her watch. She'd be late for work if she didn't hurry. She shoved the folder back in the drawer. Tomorrow. Tomorrow for sure she'd sign the papers, mail them to Brad Hensley. Then she could face Garth, tell him that it would only be a matter of waiting a few months, then she'd be free.

Eileen greeted her as she rushed in a little flushed from hurrying. "Where's Megan?" she asked.

Sometimes Val brought Megan along as Tom doted on the little girl and was always happy to have her watch TV with him or sit near him while he worked on his boat.

"Garth took her to supper at the Dock Café. They're great pals, you know."

Eileen raised her eyebrows. "I know. We've all noticed. I think Tom's a little jealous."

"You're kidding," Val said, surprised.

"Yes, of course," Eileen said, grinning. "But we're all wondering when you two are going to set a wedding date."

Val looked startled. She had no idea she and Garth had been the subject of speculation among The Seawinds folks. She glanced around to be sure none of the other waitresses who were setting up their tables could hear her, then said in a low voice, "Eileen, I haven't got my divorce yet."

It was Eileen's turn to look shocked. "You haven't? What on earth are you waiting for?"

Val had no answer for that. Eileen went on, "I thought Garth was in a hurry. He sure seemed to be when he was talking to Tom and me."

"Garth has talked to you and Tom about us?"

"Yes, he has." She patted Val's hand. "I know he thinks you're a widow. We won't say anything to make him think otherwise. When and how you tell him is up to you. But you must know he's crazy about you, Val, and nuts about Megan." She paused, then said thoughtfully, "It's probably none of my business except that I care about you and Megan. Very much. And I think Garth is a prince of a fellow. His kind of man is almost extinct these days. So my advice is don't make him wait too long."

Val knew Eileen was speaking straight from her heart with only the best of intentions. And she was going to work things out. There was plenty of time, she told herself.

Val thanked Eileen and went to get her station ready for the early diners who would arrive at five. But as she took orders, and served, she was completely preoccupied. She was just coming out of the kitchen with a tray of desserts for her first table when she saw two couples coming in the entrance. One of whom she recognized. The Talbots, her former next-door neighbors in Meadowbrook. Val almost dropped the tray. For a stark second, the two women stared at each other. Emily's face blanched. It was Val who finally gained her composure enough to say quietly, "Hello, Emily."

"Val!" Emily gasped, looking as if she'd seen a ghost.

Her husband turned a deep red when he realized who the waitress was. Jack had been one of the most verbal to condemn Kevin after his arrest. Val knew he had forbidden Emily to have any contact with her. In better days, Jack had spent a lot of time on their patio drinking Kevin's imported beer and trading jokes.

The other couple looked puzzled. They knew something strange was going on but didn't know what. Suddenly, Val knew there was nothing that could be said other than acknowledging each other. She didn't have to explain anything. There had been a time when they were as close as sisters. She and Emily had traded recipes and maternity clothes, borrowed teacups and missing baking ingredients. Now they had nothing to say to one other.

"Nice to see you," Val murmured, then moved past them to save Emily the embarrassment of introducing her to the other couple.

Later, Val chanced a look across the room and saw they were seated at another waitress's section. Somehow she got through the rest of her shift. She couldn't help but wonder what their dinner conversation had been. The neigborhood scandal starring Kevin might have provided something juicier than the steaks they'd ordered. As much as she tried to tell herself it didn't matter, Val felt keenly the old agony of lost friendships, ruined reputations and shattered lives.

When her shift ended, Val hurried outside to wait for Garth and Megan. She didn't want Emily to see either of them or Megan to see her. It would have all had to be explained and Val wanted to tell Garth about everything in her own time and place.

* * *

The season was coming to a close again. The Mc-Dermotts were getting ready for their winter vacation in Mexico. Since Labor Day the restaurant was only open on the weekends. During the week, Val worked in the office, getting all the billing done and helping with the final bookkeeping and correspondence. At the end of one morning's work, Eileen handed her a generous check.

"This is way too much," Val protested, staring at the amount.

"Nonsense. I couldn't have accomplished this much without your help. Use it for something special for yourself, Val." Her eyes twinkled merrily as she added, "But promise you won't get married until we get back. I want to give you and Garth a fabulous wedding banquet and reception."

"Oh, Eileen!" Val laughed and they hugged. She didn't mention the divorce was still not filed. She knew Eileen would be shocked at her delaying for so long. Val pushed back the nagging question in her own mind about why she hadn't yet done it. She thanked Eileen and left. Garth and Megan were waiting for her at the cove. They were going to have a cookout that evening. Val was to stop at the cottage and pack the rest of the food into a basket to bring down for their picnic supper.

As she walked home along the beach road, Val thought how especially lovely this fall had been. It was a beautiful day. The ocean stretched out in at least five shades of blue and there wasn't a cloud in the sky. Garth had said there would be a full moon that night. That meant they could stay down at the beach until late.

Val smiled to herself, looking forward to the evening ahead, as this was the nicest time to swim and then they could build a driftwood fire, toast marshmallows.... Later, she remembered that she didn't have a hint or clue that anything would mar this happy time they'd planned together.

The blue-and-white mail truck passed her on the road and she waved at the driver. She was surprised to see him stop at her mailbox. She never got any mail other than the junk marked Occupant. But before going down to the house, she stopped and checked. She found a long white envelope with a return address she immediately recognized. She shivered as she drew it out. It was from the prison chaplain. She tore the envelope open and unfolded the single typewritten sheet. Her eyes raced down the page.

It has been a long time since you have heard from me and an equally long time since I have received an inquiry from you as to your husband's progress. You will be glad to know there has been a remarkable change in your husband over the past few months. This should encourage you to try for another visit.

I have had the opportunity to discuss your last one and Kevin expresses some remorse over the way he reacted to your coming. In a number of one-on-one sessions I have been able to have with him, he feels that he has severed his relationship with you. That the divorce he demanded has erased any possibility of reconciliation.

His attitude toward rehabilitation is encourag-

ing. He has attended the group meetings regularly
and has availed himself of some self-help tapes
from the library and is working out in the gym.
In other words, I see a positive change.

I want to encourage you to keep communicating with your husband. An inmate who has a
stable relationship on the outside has a much better chance of rehabilitation and eventually apply-
ing for parole.

There was more, but Val stopped reading. Her hands
turned to ice. She walked down the dunes, slipping and
sliding as she did until she reached the front porch of
the cottage. There she sat down because her legs were
so wobbly. A dull throb began in her temple as her mind
filled with questions. Now what? Why now? Just as she
thought she was turning a corner, heading for a new life,
the past rose up and slapped her down. Kevin remorse-
ful, wanting a reconciliation? Kevin expressing regret
for his actions? All the things she'd yearned for in the
first miserable months of his imprisonment were happening now. When it was too late. Too late? For him?
For me? Too late for the wonderful things Garth was
offering? Garth! Val's hands clenched, crumpling up
the envelope.

She felt dizzy, put her head in her hands, moaning. If
only she'd signed the divorce papers, mailed them. By
now, Kevin's lawyer would have filed them. It was almost two years. It would have been final by now. Kevin
would have received his copy and they would have been
divorced. She would have been free.

The sun shifted direction and hit her eyes. Val put

up her hand to shield them. How long she'd been sitting there in a kind of daze, she didn't know. She pulled herself to her feet, hanging on to the porch post, and went inside. Moving mechanically, she packed the picnic basket, filled two thermoses, one with milk, one with coffee, put in the hot dogs, buns, mustard, relish, marshmallows, cookies. Then she changed into her bathing suit, got sweaters for both her and Megan for later, picked up towels and a blanket, stuffed them into a large canvas tote.

Before she left, she smoothed out the wrinkled envelope containing the chaplain's letter and put it in the drawer on top of the blue legal folder. Then she went out of the cottage and headed for the cove. Resolutely, she made a decision. *I'll think about this tomorrow, decide what to do tomorrow, but at least we'll have this day.*

Chapter Nineteen

Val saw Garth and Megan before they saw her. Both were standing at the water's edge. Garth was helping her with the small fishing rod he had bought for her and she was casting her line. She heard Megan's high lilting laugh and Garth's deep voice as he coached her. Val winced. Her chest felt tight with pain. How could she possibly give this up?

As she stood there watching the two of them, Val became sharply aware of the passage of time. Megan was almost seven. She had grown so much this past year. The pink bathing suit new at the start of the summer was now faded, almost too small for the long legs and little-girl skinniness that had replaced the baby plumpness of last year. It didn't seem possible that they had been at Seawood for almost two years.

Garth turned, saw her and waved, smiling. "There's your mom," he told Megan, and she turned, too.

"Look, Mommy!" She shook her fishing line, a big grin on her face.

"I see, darling!" Val called back over the lump rising in her throat. Megan was so completely happy.

It would have been a perfect evening if Val hadn't had such a heavy heart. The burden of what she had to tell Garth hung over her like a black cloud. Megan managed to stay awake long enough to see the huge pale moon rise over the sea. Then she'd been content to be wrapped in a blanket while Val and Garth remained basking in its silvery glow.

After a few minutes, Val drew a long breath, ready to tell Garth what had to be told. She knew there was no easy way to break this to him. However, before she had a chance, Garth said, "I have some great news. I didn't want to say anything about it in front of Megan until I'd checked it out first with you."

"What is it?" Val asked, glad of the temporary reprieve.

"I heard from my agent in New York today and he's negotiating a contract for illustrations for a book that's to be published both in France and this country. The bonus is that the background is to be Paris!"

"You mean you'll be going to Paris?"

"No, Val, we—you, Megan and I—will be going to Paris. For six months or maybe a year! Isn't that wonderful? We can be married and spend our honeymoon in Paris...city of lights, city of lovers!" He leaned over and kissed Val on the tip of her nose. "Well, aren't you going to say something?" he teased.

"I'm speechless," she managed to murmur.

Garth started to kiss her again, but she turned her head.

"Garth, I have to tell you something."

"Okay, but don't frown." He smiled.

"Garth, I'm serious."

"So am I. Very serious. Seriously in love." He put his arm around her shoulder to draw her close, but she stiffened.

"Please, Garth, I haven't told you the truth about something important. I know I should have long before this, but I didn't, and now I don't know where to begin."

"You haven't got a passport? Well, that's no problem. We can fix that."

Val's heart sank. Garth was so elated, this was going to be much harder than she'd thought. "Listen, it's not about passports or Paris, or maybe it is. I don't know exactly where to start."

Garth looked puzzled. "The beginning's usually a good place. But, Val, don't feel you have to tell me anything about your past you'd rather not. I don't want to know anything that's going to make you unhappy."

"It does make me unhappy, but you've got to know. We can't make any plans. At least not right away. I should have told you before this. You see, I'm not free to marry you."

A blankness came over Garth's expression as if what Val had said didn't register. He looked at her as if she'd been speaking a foreign language.

"I'm not a widow like you assumed, like I told you." Val swallowed hard but continued. "My husband is in prison. He's serving a sentence for embezzlement. He wanted me to divorce him, but I never did. I just couldn't bring myself to do it. He wanted me to build a new life for myself and Megan, move from the community where we'd lived, where we were known. That's how I happened to come here, why I used my maiden name. He didn't want to see me, to communicate in any way. I went once. He was furious with me. Since then we haven't—I haven't seen or heard from him for over a year."

She stopped, took a long, shaky breath. "Then I met you. It changed my life. I was so lonely, desperately lonely. But I never dreamed we'd…fall in love, that we had any kind of future together." A sob broke her voice. "Oh, Garth, I'm so terribly sorry. I should have told you long before this. It was wrong not to. I guess I was afraid…."

The tears came then and the racking sobs. Garth's arms went around Val, cradling her against him. His hand smoothed the back of her head as it lay on his shoulder, his voice soft, comforting, as he soothed her. "It doesn't matter, darling. Don't cry, please. It's all right. It's going to be all right. You can still go ahead, get your divorce. Here in California it only takes a matter of weeks. Everything can be taken care of and then we can get married."

Sniffling, Val pulled away. "Oh, Garth, if only it was that simple. There's more. I got a letter from the prison chaplain. Kevin has changed his mind about wanting Megan and me out of his life. His whole attitude has changed…he's working in the programs with the goal of getting paroled." She gulped back more sobs. "The chaplain says it's important for an inmate to have the possibility of returning to a stable home, loving relatives. It will go a long way in impressing the parole board to grant Kevin a parole."

Garth was silent, his face set in grim lines.

"The chaplain says if Kevin knows I'm waiting for him, it will make all the difference."

"But that's unfair. Why should you be sacrificed? The man kicked you out of his life, forced you to start over, work at a job you weren't prepared for, struggle along bringing Megan up alone. Now, he can't expect to have everything again. Just because he needs you to get out of prison."

"It's not exactly like that, Garth. Kevin hasn't contacted me himself. It was the chaplain who wrote—"

Garth was bristling with anger. "Who is this guy to tell you what you should do with your life?"

"He's just a man trying to do his job. Help prisoners get their lives back together."

"What about you? What about me? Are you going to let a letter from some guy we don't even know change everything? Unless..." Garth hesitated as if he could hardly bring himself to ask the question. "Or do you still love your husband?"

Val flung her hands out helplessly. "Love? Not the way you mean. I did what he wanted me to even though I didn't think it was right. But you can't just wipe out twelve years of your life as though they never existed." She paused. "I care what happens to him. Yes."

Megan stirred, murmured in her sleep. Garth leaned over and pulled the blanket more securely around her. Then he turned back to Val. "Does she know about this?"

Val shook her head. "No. She rarely talks about Kevin anymore. A child forgets soon. He never wrote or anything. I just told her Daddy had gone away. Kevin used to travel a lot. She was used to it just being the two of us. Certainly now she is. Except that now she has you, too."

Garth got up abruptly and stalked down to the ocean's edge. Val could see his tall figure silhouetted against the silvery moonlight, the ocean a rippling, glittering backdrop. Then she thought of Kevin. No matter what she did, everyone was going to be hurt.

Garth walked back and forth for a long time. Then he came back to Val. He sat down beside her again and gently took her hands in his. "We don't have to talk about this anymore tonight. We'll sleep on it. Then we can decide what you'll do."

Silently, they gathered everything up. Repacked the picnic basket, folded the blanket, towels. Then Garth lifted Megan and carried her up the beach, over the dunes and into the cottage. Val followed him, set down the basket, the other things. Garth came out of Megan's bedroom where he had laid her gently on the bed. He came over to Val, took her into his arms and held her for a long time. She could feel his heart beating against hers and she closed her eyes, wishing none of this had happened, wishing...wishing... She sighed. Remembered the song from an old movie. "A wish is a dream your heart makes." If she could just wish them all into her dream of happily ever after...

Garth's voice brought her back to reality. "Nothing has to be decided right away. I have some work to get out in the morning, but I'll come over later. Things will look better in the morning, you'll see. We can talk then."

She looked up at him and nodded. Then he left. Drained of all emotion, Val lay down on the couch in the front room. Garth had made it sound as if what she did would be a joint decision. But she knew, in her deepest heart of hearts, that it had to be her decision and hers alone.

Chapter Twenty

"Mommy, why are you sleeping out here?" Megan's anxious little face close to hers awakened Val. She raised herself on her elbows, pushed back her hair and tried to focus sleep-heavy eyes to look at the child peering down at her.

"I guess I just drifted off out here, honey." Val sat up. She pulled herself to her feet, feeling cold and stiff, her neck aching from the awkward position in which she had finally fallen asleep. Slowly, the agonizing scene with Garth came back to her. Her mind felt fuzzy. What had she decided? Then she remembered. Nothing. It was all still a terrible unsolved muddle.

Megan skipped out to the kitchen area, calling back over her shoulder, "Are we going to the cove again today, Mommy? You said we could."

Val heard the sound of the kitchen stool being moved, cabinet doors opening then slamming shut, the clatter of dishes and the rustle of dry cereal being poured into a bowl.

"Can I have cocoa for breakfast? I can make it myself." The refrigerator door clicked and Megan's voice continued. "Guess what, Mommy? Bonnie's cat is going to have kittens and she said I could have one of them when they get bornded. Is that okay with you? I'd like a gray striped one like the mama cat. Except her four paws are white. That's why they call her Boots."

Val clenched her teeth. The sound of Megan's sweet, high voice was grating on her pounding head. Her impulse was to beg Megan to play quietly with her dolls in her room for the morning, allow her to get some more sleep. But with the need to make a decision hanging over her, Val knew she probably couldn't sleep anyway. Out in the kitchen, she groped in the cabinet over the sink for the bottle of aspirin and gulped down two while trying to oversee Megan measuring cocoa powder into a saucepan and adding milk from the carton without spilling it all over the counter.

"So can we, Mommy?" Megan persisted.

"Can we what, honey?"

"Go to our cove."

"Oh, yes, I guess so." Every nerve in Val's body longed for peace and quiet to think, to plan, to come to some conclusion.

She made herself some strong coffee and sipped it standing at the window. The whole coast was a misty gray-green, but even as she watched, the thin veil lifted and a bright sun came out, revealing the long stretch of beach. It was going to be another beautiful day after all. Maybe it would be a good thing to be down at the cove.

Their cove was tucked between large, overhanging cliffs; a crescent of sandy beach curved from the dunes. The rocks formed natural tunnels that filled rapidly when the tide was coming in. This morning, the tide was out, leaving a wide margin of wet gray surface, perfect for sand-castle building. Driftwood and kelp were strewn on the beach swept up from the last high tide.

Val felt as though she was moving in slow motion as she staggered up over the dunes and got settled with the blanket spread out, the picnic basket and thermoses. By the time she had stretched out on her stomach, her chin on folded arms so that she could watch Megan, the little girl was already filling her bucket with water.

Val thought of the day before when all three of them had been down here together. Without Garth, something was definitely missing. What was she going to do? The things that had kept her awake most of the night now seemed to be slipping out of her grasp. She felt too weary to figure out anything. The scene at the prison when she'd visited Kevin rose up in vivid detail. She saw his face, twisted with bitterness, eyes shuttered with resentment, his whole body bristling with anger. Could he have changed? Really changed, as the chaplain indicated? Val shuddered even though the sun was prickling her back with hot needles.

Then she thought of Garth, of the wonderful future he was offering them. She squinted her eyes against the sun's glare, looked down to the water's edge where Megan squatted on the shoreline. Almost as if aware of her mother's gaze, the little girl turned and waved. Val waved back. Megan loved Garth. He would be such a great father.... *Oh, dear God, how can I make the right choice?* Any choice she made would hurt someone. Who had the most claim on her? Megan? Garth? Kevin?

The answer that came seemed to lead her—drag her—down a dead-end road she had traveled before.

Back to a time of waiting, of being unable to see whatever was at the end of it. There was no guarantee that Kevin would be paroled even if she did stay with him. If she gave up a new life with Garth, Kevin might still have to serve his entire sentence, and then what? She would have lost the chance for a kind of happiness she knew now she had always wanted but never imagined was possible. And she would have lost it for Megan, too.

The sun playing on the water was dazzlingly bright. Far out on the horizon, a freighter moved slowly. The surf swirled in foamy circles onto the sand with a measured rhythm. Val felt her eyelids grow heavier, droop. The need for sleep was almost overpowering. She glanced at Megan now industriously piling mounds of sand into a huge pyramid. Val blinked and stifled a yawn. The urge to close her eyes was irresistible. She put her head down on her folded arms, thinking it would be for just a minute.

Suddenly, she jerked her head up. Shivering, she sat up. The sun had shifted and she was now completely in shadow. The wind off the ocean was cool. Wide awake, she got to her knees, then stood. Megan was nowhere in sight. A jolt like an electric shock went through her when she saw the empty beach, saw Megan's sand castle collapsing in the wake of the inrushing tide.

"Megan! Megan!" she shouted. But her voice was carried away by the roar of the waves. She ran forward, stumbling in the softer sand of the dunes, down to the beach where Megan was playing just a few minutes ago.

A few minutes? Had she been asleep for twenty minutes or more? Panic gripped her. Could Megan possibly have been swept out to sea? Had she been kneeling, her back to the ocean, been caught by a wave she didn't see? *Oh, dear God,* Val silently screamed, *I shouldn't have taken my eyes off her, not for one second.*

She waded into the water, calling Megan's name, the waves lapping around her calves, then her knees. Her child's name became a frantic sob. "Oh, God, please, God, don't let anything have happened to Megan...."

Just then from behind her, she heard, "Mommy, Mommy, here I am!"

Val whirled around, nearly losing her balance in the pull of the strong current. Then she saw her. Megan was standing on top of one of the rocks on the shelf of bluffs above the cove. How she had ever climbed up that far, Val didn't know. But the fact was, she was there. Val ran through the surf, gesturing wildly, calling, "Megan, don't! It's too high up there. Come down."

But Megan only waved and turned back, continuing to climb. With a sense of horror, Val realized the little girl couldn't hear her. Megan was usually obedient. She wouldn't have deliberately disobeyed her mother. She just didn't know how dangerous the cliffs were. She had thought it was an adventure. Something out of *Swiss Family Robinson,* the abbreviated edition Garth was now illustrating and reading to Megan. She had been captivated by the daring exploits of the children of the shipwrecked family. That's probably what was in her mind when she ventured up the steep slope. Val knew she didn't realize that she would have to come down, the descent just as perilous as the climb had been.

Concentrating on trying to get Megan's attention, Val was unaware of her own situation until she felt a pulling rush of water from under her feet, the sucking sensation of the waves on her bare legs. The tide was coming in fast. Just as this realization hit, a hard wave knocked her down and there was a swirl of sand and shells. Grappling for a foothold, she struggled to get back up but only half succeeded when another big wave struck.

Gasping for breath, Val tried to run into shore but was caught as the wave broke, hitting her hard and sending her down as the water rushed over her in a thundering crash. On her hands and knees now, she managed to crawl then stagger to her feet and make the shore before another incoming wave could wash over her. Her palms and knees were scraped by sharp pieces of shell. But that didn't matter. All that mattered was getting Megan down safely and then getting away from the cove before the tide came in and cut off their escape.

At last she made it to the bottom of the cliff. Yelling at the top of her voice, she called again, "Megan, Megan, come down at once. The tide's coming in. We've got to hurry and get out before we get caught."

Megan turned with a look on her face that stopped Val from saying anything else.

"I can't, Mommy!" she wailed.

"What do you mean, you can't?"

"I'm scared. It's too high. It's too far down."

Val bit her lip. Out of her own fear, she nearly said, You should have thought of that. Of course, she didn't. As slowly and calmly as she could manage, Val directed, "Stay right there. Don't move. I'll come get you."

There was no time to argue, no time to hesitate. Soon the narrow channel leading to the other side of the beach would be filled with the churning ocean water sweeping in with the tide.

Chilled from her soaking and urged on by fear, Val ran over to their things and shoved her feet into her thongs. They weren't climbing boots but would be better than trying to cover the rocks in her bare feet. She ran back to the foot of the cliff. She could hear Megan crying now. The little girl had realized her predicament. Val called up to her, "Don't worry, honey. I'm coming, just hold on."

Slowly, Val picked her way up the rocks, breaking a couple of fingernails as she grasped for handholds to pull herself up. Above, Megan's crying got louder.

Val tried to soothe her. "Don't move, Megan. I'm coming." At last she reached the little girl and Megan flung herself on Val, nearly toppling them both. "Wait, honey, we're going to have to go piggyback. That's the only way Mommy can climb down and carry you."

Val swiveled, holding on to Megan until the little girl was positioned on her back, her legs straddling Val's waist, her arms in a strangling grip around Val's shoulders and neck.

"You're choking me, honey!" Val pleaded at one point. But Megan's clasp didn't loosen. The child was too frightened. Somehow, Val never knew how, they inched their way down the cliff. The feel of sand on her feet was welcome. She set Megan down gently and looked around. The waves were higher and coming in with increasing speed. "Come on, Megan, we've got to make a run for it. Grab everything you can. Then let's go."

The water was getting deep as they waded through

the arch formed by the gigantic boulders that served as the entrance to the cove. Val held tight to Megan's hand with her one hand, carrying their picnic basket in the other, the blanket over her arm. Megan was carrying one of the thermoses, but as the waves churned under their feet, she dropped it and it disappeared in the waves. "It doesn't matter," Val told her, pulling her along.

At last they reached the beach on the other side, and with a safe expanse of sand between them and the incoming tide, Val stopped to catch her breath, and reassemble their belongings. Megan was shivering violently. Her lips were blue. Val wrapped the blanket around her, but it was damp and didn't give her much warmth.

"Come on, darling, we'll have to hurry and get home. We'll pop you in a warm bath right away or you'll catch a terrible cold. Try to run, okay?"

Just as they were struggling up the last few feet of the dunes in front of the cottage, Megan tugged on Val's hand and said plaintively, "I'm sorry, Mommy."

Val's heart melted. "It's okay, darling, we've both learned a lesson. Once you've had a bath and some hot chocolate, we'll both feel better."

A half hour later, Megan was bundled up in front of the stove, both hands clutching a mug of creamy cocoa. It was only then Val realized *she* was still in her wet bathing suit, her hair dripping. The supply in their small hot water tank had nearly run out by the time she got into the tub herself, and instead of warming her, the tepid water chilled her more.

No matter what she tried—cups of steaming tea, changing into a warm sweater, wool slacks—Val couldn't seem to get warm. Along with the outer shivering, an inner trembling began. It was the belated realization of the danger both Megan and she had been in that day.

She was still cold, yet feverish, when late in the afternoon, Garth showed up. When she told him what had happened, he frowned. "You mean you think Megan didn't hear you at first?"

"I called and called, then when she realized where she was, she turned and looked down. That's when she saw me. I'm not sure she heard me before then."

"Do you think her deafness is getting worse? I thought I noticed it, too, but I wasn't sure. Her not hearing you could be dangerous. More dangerous than today." Garth's frown deepened. "Maybe we should make an appointment with a specialist, have her checked. Possibly some kind of hearing aid would help."

Val's heart turned over. Garth had said "we" as if it was both their responsibility. Garth was so dear, so concerned. His love for Megan was apparent. She covered his hand with her own. "Yes, maybe we should. I feel so guilty. I should never have gone to sleep. Taken my eyes off her."

"It's all this unnecessary tension—that letter, all of it has upset you. You're not yourself. Not thinking straight. No wonder…" His mouth grew grimly tight. Val knew he was suppressing a lot of what he was feeling, thinking.

She was now beginning to feel too ill to talk about what was foremost in both their minds. It would be no use to go into it any further tonight. Although she protested she'd be all right, Garth insisted she go to bed.

He would take care of Megan, feed her supper, read to her and tuck her in, which Megan was delighted to hear. Gratefully, Val agreed and left them to go to bed.

She woke in the middle of the night aching in every bone, with a throbbing head and a heaviness in her chest. The next morning when Garth arrived to check on them, she could only speak in a hoarse whisper. There was no question but that she should remain in bed. Garth took over. He brought lemons, vitamin C tablets and chicken broth. Then he took Megan to school. He also called Val's manager at the hardware store, where she had resumed her job from last winter, and told him that Val was ill and unable to come to work. He reappeared every hour or so and Val was only vaguely aware of his coming and going. She slept deeply, grateful that Garth was in charge, glad to relinquish Megan's care to him, too weak to feel any guilt.

Two days later, Val woke up clearheaded and rested. She heard the sound of movement in the kitchen area and Megan's and Garth's voices. Soon Garth appeared at her bedroom door with a tray. "Good morning, sleepyhead." He grinned. "Feeling better?"

"Yes, thanks to you. I think I might live." Val sat up, pushed her pillow behind her back. "How can I ever repay you for this, Garth? It was beyond the call of duty or friendship or anything." She shook her head. "You were wonderful taking care of me and Megan like this."

"Don't you know that's what I want to do? Keep on doing? Taking care of you and Megan for the rest of our lives?"

His words brought back the fact of the letter from the prison chaplain. The one that had brought about their crisis before she became ill. Now, as their eyes met in a loving gaze, Val remembered. She drew back the hand she had held out to Garth.

His smile faded as if he knew what had happened. He set down the tray on her lap, then drew an envelope out of his shirt pocket and laid it alongside her cup and saucer. "This came in yesterday's mail."

Val glanced at the return address and recognized the handwriting. It was Kevin's. She looked up at Garth.

"I'll take Megan to school. Give you a chance to read this in private. When I get back, we can talk."

The little house seemed unnaturally still after they left. Or maybe Val's heart was pounding so loudly so that it silenced every other sound. Blocked everything out while she opened Kevin's letter.

It was written in his familiar style. Staccato sentences, lots of dashes.

Dear Val,

I'm not sure I'll have the guts to mail this when I finish writing it—not after all I've done and put you through—but the chaplain and the prison shrink both think it will be therapeutic for me to do this—and who am I to argue with them?

I understand the chaplain has been in touch with you over the past year and he thinks you may be willing to forgive and forget. I don't know if this is true or not—I wouldn't blame you if it isn't. But I've always been one to take a risk. So I guess that's what this letter is—a gamble.

I've been going to the group encounter sessions. They're pretty rough. Nobody lets you get away with anything. Everyone says what they think. The counselor who leads the group says the seeds of how we turn out are sown early in our lives, the reasons why we act like we do, do the things that get us in here. Not that I'm like most of the other guys. My childhood wasn't rougher than some of theirs. I had a lot going for me at one time. I just got off track somewhere. It might have all worked out. But that's another story.

The real point of this letter is to tell you I do care about you and Megan—whatever I might have said—whatever you might have been led to believe.

I want you to know I'm not counting on anything—and I'm not holding you to anything. I know you didn't sign the divorce papers even though I thought that's what I wanted you to do, told you to do. The chaplain says that means something—does it, Val? Maybe things could work out for us if I get released early, get a parole—the chaplain says there's a good chance of that. First offense—no prior record—I'm turning into a model prisoner. How about that? The point is that an inmate who toes the line—follows the rules—that's considered good conduct in here.

The big thing is if a man has a stable home life on the outside, there's a real chance for rehabilitation—that he won't repeat the offense he's serving time for. That kind of guy is much more likely to get a parole. These prisons are overcrowded with real criminals—they'd like to get rid of some of the ones who are not a danger to society. Any-

way, if you still have any love left in your heart
for me, we could start over and be together as a
family again—I'm hoping this is how it is. It's
up to you, Val. I won't blame you if you've had
it but I thought you'd want to know I've changed
my mind—about a lot of things. Well, I guess
that's all for now.

Yours ever,
Kevin

Val let the letter drop out of limp hands, leaned her
head back against the pillow and closed her eyes. The
man who had written this letter was a new Kevin. Kevin
was never the kind to look at himself, to examine his
motives or explain his actions. Reading this letter, Val
thought of how hopeless she'd sometimes felt in their
marriage. How she could rarely express her real feelings. She recalled all the hurts and misunderstandings,
the times she'd been filled with resentment, angered by
Kevin's indifference toward her or Megan. Now he was
bringing into the open some of the things they'd never
talked about. Why had it taken this terrible experience
to make him see reality?

Val knew the letter had at least accomplished one
thing. It had brought her to a decision. She had to go and
see Kevin again. See this new Kevin. Judge for herself
if this was for real. Maybe discover what she could not
read between the scrawled lines of this letter.

Time had not blotted out hurtful memories, all she
had been forced to face, handle, manage on her own.
It had been nearly two years. If Kevin had changed,
so had she. They were no longer the same two people

they had been. The question was, how much had they changed? Were there now irreconcilable differences— as the divorce petition stated—for them to be together ever again?

Val had to find out. Before she made any other decision. She would have to see Kevin. The only thing she dreaded was telling Garth.

Chapter Twenty-One

They didn't have a chance to talk until early that evening. It wasn't until after Garth had fixed them all supper, Megan had been read to and tucked in bed. Wrapped in a blanket, Val was propped on the couch in front of the stove, where the fire Garth had built earlier crackled cheerfully.

As gently and as reasonably as she could, Val broke the news that she had decided to visit Kevin again. That she felt compelled to do so. Garth's reaction was what she had expected.

"Why did this have to happen now? We were so happy." His jaw set, he leaned forward clenching his hands.

Val longed to reach over, comfort him in some way, but she didn't dare touch him. Her own emotions were too precarious. It would only make things harder. She knew now what she had to do. "I have to go. Don't you see that?"

"If you feel that's what you have to do, of course." Then Garth said firmly, "But you're not going anywhere until you're completely well."

"I know. Besides, I'll have to write first, find out when I can come, the visiting schedule, that sort of thing." What she didn't mention was her own determination to be careful not to give Kevin any false hope.

Another silence followed. Garth kept staring at the fire. Val watched the light from the flickering firelight cast interesting shadows on the rugged contours of his face. Garth cleared his throat as if what he was going to say was difficult. He turned toward her.

A muscle in Garth's cheek tightened visibly. "I don't want you to go."

"I know, but there's no other way. I'd never have any peace if I didn't."

Garth pounded his fist into his palm. "*Why?* I keep asking myself *why*."

"It's all my fault," Val said miserably. "I should have told you about Kevin, told you the whole truth right from the start. Then none of this would have happened."

"No, sweetheart." Garth was beside her in a second, kneeling on the floor. He took both her hands in his and looked at her. "It isn't your fault. My falling in love with you would have happened anyway. Something started the first time I saw you and then when I met you again, that day on the beach." He shook his head vigorously. "No, you and I, we were meant to be. I thought so then. I still think so. I'm tired of all this talk, this confusion we're feeling. It's not fair and it's not right. No matter what, I'll go on loving you."

Val touched his cheek with her hand, relishing his strength. She pushed away her guilty feelings. If only she'd done what Kevin wanted in the first place. Now she would be free. Free to love Garth. But fair or not—

and whoever said life was fair?—the promises she'd made to Kevin still stood. Slowly she moved away from Garth, walked over to the window and looked out. How calm the sea looked today, unlike her own troubled soul.

Ten days passed and Val moved through them like a sleepwalker. On the surface, things were the same although she and Garth treated each other with extra gentleness, extra consideration. Val meticulously avoided any physical contact with Garth. She knew Garth was exerting the same control. They waited, like two people on the precipice of a mountain, for word from the prison. When it came, there was a feeling of anguished relief. At least now they had a time and a date.

When Val showed Garth the letter she had received back from the chaplain, he read it, then looked at her, his deep-set eyes full of anxiety. Impulsively, Val put her hand over his. "Oh, Garth, I'm so sorry for what this is doing to you. I've really messed up your life, haven't I?"

"Don't say that. Don't even think that." He frowned.

"But it's true. You would have been so much better off falling in love with someone with a less complicated life."

"Val, I love you. There couldn't be anyone else."

"Hasn't there ever been?" Val asked.

From the first, they had simply taken each other at face value. Val had avoided talking about her own past, did not want to answer questions Garth might ask, and so had been afraid to ask Garth about his. Naturally, she had wondered about it. Someone as attractive and interesting as Garth must have had a past, must have seen other women.

He had no reticence about it. He was forthright and casual as he told her, "Of course. In college, like everyone else. They were short-lived romances. Then I was so intent on my career there wasn't really time for a serious relationship. When that got underway, there were times when I was attracted to someone. Once or twice it even looked like it might lead somewhere. Then I'd find I was saying a lot of things I didn't mean, going places I didn't like, doing things I wasn't much interested in doing." He paused, a slight smile lifting the corners of his mouth. "At the risk of being really corny, can I tell you I think I've been searching for someone like you all my life?"

Val smiled at him with a kind of wistfulness. "Maybe a little corny, but very nice."

Things moved very quickly after Val got the letter stating Kevin was looking forward to her visit. But what to do about Megan for the two days it would take traveling back and forth? Val knew the only way would be to take the McDermotts into her confidence again.

If Garth's reaction could have been anticipated, Eileen's was even more negative. "But why now of all times? I thought you and Garth were making plans. Why jeopardize your future, yours and Megan's?"

"I have to go, Eileen. I know it's hard for anyone else to understand. But that's the way it is."

Eileen pressed her lips together. "My grown children tell me I shouldn't give unsolicited advice, but, Val, I really feel this is a mistake." When Val made no reply, Eileen sighed. "Okay. I've said all I'm going to say. And of course we'll keep Megan. Does she know where you're going and why?"

"No, I want to wait and see if...well, see and talk to Kevin first. I'll just have to cross that bridge when I come to it." Val knew that was an unsatisfactory answer but the only one she could give right now.

She decided not to say anything to her daughter about her father. Not just yet. So much hung in the balance. She would know what to do or not to do after she'd seen Kevin.

The night before Val was to leave, Garth went with her to take Megan to the McDermotts. Then they drove over to Oceanview and went to a small Italian restaurant for dinner. Neither of them had much of an appetite nor ate very much. They talked very little, just gazed at each other across the candlelit table, heart-heavy with all that was unspoken. Afterward, they returned to the beach practically in silence. Garth parked on the road above Val's cottage. He cut the engine, then turned to her. Without a word, she touched his cheek with her hand. Then she flung open the door and ran up the path, her vision blurred by tears.

Chapter Twenty-Two

The next day as Val waited for the bus out to the prison, everything seemed strangely familiar. I've done this before, Val thought with a sense of the ridiculous bordering on hysteria that she knew was inappropriate.

But everything was exactly the same as the first time she'd made this trip to visit Kevin. Even though this time he was expecting her, wanted her to come, Val had the same panicky sensation. She felt the perspiration gathering on her hands, felt the frightening breathlessness, the terrifying pounding of her heart. She felt sandy-eyed from not having enough sleep.

She had not been able to sleep last night either in the cheap motel where she'd checked in upon her arrival. When she gave up trying after a night of tossing and turning, she had showered and dressed.

She started to pin the small jeweled ladybug pin Garth had given her at Christmas on the lapel of her cornflower blue jacket. Then decided not to. Kevin might ask questions. He always noticed such things. She held it in her hand for a few seconds, then slipped it into her handbag. It made her feel unhappy to do it. As if she was abandoning Garth.

She went out into the early-morning stillness of the street. Besides the bus station, the only place open where she could get a cup of coffee was a diner. Inside its white tiled interior, the glaring fluorescent lights burned into her sleep-hungry eyes. She forced herself to nibble on a stale sweet roll and swallow a little coffee. Then she went back to her motel room to wait out the next two hours before it was time to catch the prison bus.

Again she was struck by the sight of the others waiting for the bus. Bound together on this common journey yet separated by private pain. There was an older woman with sad, dark eyes carrying a covered wicker basket, which, Val knew from her previous visit, she would not be allowed to carry into the visitors' section. It was probably filled with nothing more than home-baked goodies, perhaps favorites of the man she was coming to see. However, it would be checked for drugs or anything that might be made into a weapon. It might never reach the person for whom the contents had been baked so lovingly. Val glanced at the woman sympathetically. Whoever she was visiting—husband, brother, son—he had done his share of etching the deep lines in her face.

Suddenly, a thought struck Val. How would she look in fifteen years? How would she seem to younger women waiting to go up to that gray stone fortress on the hill? A wave of nausea swept over her. But she managed to control it. She looked away quickly and saw the bus coming.

She maneuvered the high step carefully, thinking she had been foolish to wear high heels. She had done so automatically, remembering that Kevin had always pre-ferred her to wear them. What difference did it make? The point of her coming was not to please Kevin. But as they neared the bus stop near the prison gate, she took out her compact and checked her image.

Kevin would find her changed. The hairstyle, the color, all different. Still tanned from the summer, she wore much less makeup now. No eyeliner and only lip gloss. She liked the way she looked, felt it was her real self. Maybe that was one of the biggest changes in her. She wasn't trying to create someone else's image of how she should look or dressing to please anyone but herself these days. For the first time in years she felt she knew who she really was. And she liked it that way. A smile touched her lips. Garth seemed to like it, too.

Val also knew there were changes in her that had nothing to do with how she looked. She snapped the compact shut. With a screech of brakes, the bus jerked to a stop and the door swung open. At the gated en-trance, an armed guard checked identity cards, then in a single, silent file the visitors were let inside the com-pound to make their way to the next guarded station.

Since Val had a pass to see Chaplain Scott as well as to visit an inmate, she was led past the visitors' room, down several corridors, through several bolted doors. Her teeth clenched as she waited for a guard to unlock each one, then afterward she heard it clang and the bolt shoved back.

She was ushered into a drab little office with a cou-ple of golden oak armchairs and a window with heavy steel mesh obscuring the view, then told to wait. She tried to relax by taking deep breaths, flexing her fingers. But her hands were so moist she had to keep wiping them on her skirt.

"Mrs. Evans?" a pleasant male voice said, and Val jumped. "Sorry, I didn't mean to startle you. I'm Chaplain Scott."

Val stood up, dropping her purse as she put out her hand to shake his extended one. There followed a few minutes of confusion as they both bent to pick it up, retrieve the spilled contents.

"Won't you please sit down?" The chaplain pulled up the other chair and seated himself, smiling at her as if theirs was an ordinary kind of visit. Not a matter of life or death.

Val looked at the man whose letter had brought her here, made such an impact on the life she had made for herself since her last visit to the prison. The man who had evidently had such an influence on Kevin.

He was not handsome, his chin too prominent, his nose too large, his hair balding.

But his eyes were extraordinary, light blue, almost luminous, and he looked directly at her as he spoke. These were truth-seeking eyes, truth-telling ones. Instinctively, Val knew she could trust whatever this man said, whatever he told her. She tensed as he began to speak.

"I want you to understand that a possibility of your husband's parole is just that, a possibility. It's a long process and requires a lot of recommendations for the applicant. The one that has a great deal of bearing on whether an inmate is granted parole is what will happen when he gets out. If there's a chance of returning to old companions, old haunts, old temptations, his chances are not very good." Chaplain Scott paused significantly. "However, if he'll be returning to a loving home, a good environment, people who care about him and will support him in turning over a new leaf, well, then, it improves the likelihood of his getting paroled."

His keen gaze lingered on Val. She twisted the straps of the purse in her lap.

"The board only meets three times a year, and since they just met last month, it will be another four before they hear any new appeals. Another test of patience. Think you're up to that?"

"I don't know," Val said. "I honestly don't. It's a new idea. I'll have to wait until I see Kevin, talk to him myself."

"I don't mean to probe, but I can see you don't have the same attitude you had before. From your letter, I got the impression you were willing to wait for Kevin no matter how long it took. Have things changed? Have your feelings for your husband changed?"

Val couldn't lie. Not with those honest eyes looking penetratingly at her, as if they could see into her very heart.

"No, not exactly. I mean, I hoped Kevin was adjusting better, accepting the situation, but…yes, I guess you'd have to say things have changed. It's been almost two years. On my own a good part of that time, I've had to change." She took a long breath. "And I've met someone. Someone who means a great deal to me now. We met when I'd lost all hope that Kevin wanted us…me and our little girl. He didn't answer any of my letters."

Again Val took a breath that was almost a gasp before she went on. "A wonderful man, a good, intelligent, caring person, wants to marry me. He would provide a secure home and be a loving father to Megan."

She let this sink in for a moment before going on. The chaplain was leaning forward, listening attentively.

"The problem is, I never did what Kevin demanded at first. That I divorce him. Somehow I could never bring myself to sign the papers so that they could be filed and end our marriage."

"What does that tell you? About your own feelings? About the divorce?"

"That legally I'm still Kevin's wife, that I'm not free to marry."

"I wish I'd known this before I sent that letter," Chaplain Scott said thoughtfully. "I wouldn't have got Kevin's hopes up, encouraged him to write to you."

"He thinks everything is the same?"

"Well, he's pretty sure of it. He told me you were high school sweethearts, that your relationship has always been a good one..." The chaplain hesitated. "What does the other man think of all this?"

"He's upset, of course."

"And your little girl? Does she know there's a possibility of her daddy coming home?"

"No, I haven't told her anything." Quick tears came into Val's eyes. "I wanted to wait until things were clearer." She flung out her hands helplessly. "I don't know what to do. What's right or what's wrong. Whatever choice I make, somebody will be hurt." She looked at Chaplain Scott. "What do you think I should do?"

"I can't make that choice for you, my dear. What con-

cerns me is Kevin. If he finds out you're not willing to
provide him the support he needs to get a parole, that
you won't be waiting for him when he gets out, whenever that is, it will be a blow. A real setback." Chaplain
Scott looked grieved. "He has placed a great deal on his
belief that you still love him. I don't know what finding out that someone has taken his place in your affec-
tions and in your little girl's, well…" He shook his head.

"But is it right to penalize us for what he's brought
on himself? It just isn't fair."

"Life seldom is," Chaplain Scott said sadly.

Val got up, walked over to the window and looked
out through the mesh. She could see the corner of the
prison yard where the inmates took their exercise or
mingled in the short recreation time. Beyond were the
towering granite walls, the coiled rolls of barbed wire
and an electric fence. Beyond them were the rolling
California hills, still covered with golden poppies and
purple lupins. Beyond all this was freedom. Her freedom. To love and live unafraid, cherished, protected by
a wonderful man. She felt a wrenching desire to take
that freedom. To run out of this grim place and never
look back.

But she knew she couldn't. If Megan was her only
consideration, there would be no contest. Garth was
clearly the more sensible choice of a father for her child.
His gentleness, his interest and patience, his concern
for Megan, were so much greater than Kevin had ever
shown. But for Kevin, Val's feeling was less analyti-
cal. He had been a part of her life ever since she was
fifteen.…

Why now did the words of the wedding vows they

had taken come back to haunt her? Even though they had been spoken in the gaudy atmosphere of a Las Vegas marriage mill, to Val they had eternal meaning. She and Kevin had been joined together "in the sight of God" in a union that was to last forever, come what may, no matter what.

Val turned back from the window, faced Chaplain Scott. He was sitting, head bent forward, chin resting on folded hands, almost in a pose of prayer. Had he been praying? she wondered.

"I'm ready now, I think," she said.

"You've made your choice, then." It was more a statement than a question. He must have known, Val thought, that I never really had a choice. Maybe that was why she'd never signed the divorce papers. Somehow, underneath it all, she knew it would take more than her signature for her and Kevin's marriage to be over.

Chaplain Scott rose to his feet. "Good. Come on, I'll take you to Kevin."

They had only fifteen minutes together because this was not a regular visiting day. Kevin had to be released from his work detail in order to see Val. As Val saw her husband approach accompanied by a guard, Val thought he looked physically better than the last time. He'd been working out in the prison gym, and even in the baggy jumpsuit he wore, he looked trimmer, his bearing more energetic.

Through the glass enclosure, Val saw the look of hope in his eyes as he picked up the communicating phone.

"It was good of you to come, Val," he said.

"I wanted to see you."

"You got my letter?"

"Yes, that's why I'm here."

"Forgive me?"

She waved her hand as if that was unnecessary. There was no point in responding to that.

"How's Megan?" he asked next.

"She's doing well."

"I guess she's grown a lot. How about sending a picture?"

"Sure. They took them at school in the spring."

"You're looking good, Val. Good? You look wonderful." Kevin bit his lower lip, leaned closer to the glass. "It's so great to see you, Val. When I get out of here, I'll make it up to you."

Val felt a clutch at her heart. How could he make up for what was lost? Ever?

But Kevin rushed on, "Val, I've got so many plans. Did Chaplain Scott tell you there's a really good chance I can get paroled? Well, when I do, I have some fantastic ideas…"

Val realized the chaplain was right. Kevin was already building a larger-than-life picture of what it was going to be like when he got out. Dangerous? Maybe. But she knew it was his way of surviving. Without dreams, without big ideas, or if his hopes were dashed in here, Kevin would die.

Still, it frightened Val to see that glimpse of the old scheming Kevin, the Kevin who wanted to get the best of everything, of everybody, whatever it took.

There really wasn't much more to be said between them. Val felt the words she spoke, the replies she made, were all automatic, on the surface. The real things were too deep, too heartbreaking, too important to say in this environment. Then time was up. She had to leave.

"Will you come again?" Kevin asked.

"I'll try."

The bus ride back to Seawood passed in a sort of peculiar blur. Val felt as if she were viewing a TV program, scenes of the prison, the interview with the chaplain, then her brief visit with Kevin, superimposed on the fleeting landscape. Over and over she reviewed that strange yet hauntingly familiar time with Kevin. A Kevin subtly changed by his prison experience, yet basically the same. Her own reaction was detached. She didn't feel anything. Not love, not resentment, not bitterness, only a kind of emptiness within.

For some reason, the bus pulled into Seawood forty minutes ahead of its scheduled arrival. She had called Garth from a phone booth before boarding the bus so he could meet her. His voice, tight, tense, had asked, "How did things go?"

"I'll tell you when I see you," she had replied. And hung up. She hadn't wanted to go into anything on the phone. She wanted to wait until she could tell him face-to-face.

She got off the bus and looked around. There was no sign of Garth. Of course, it was earlier than he'd expected her. All at once, Val felt terrified. She couldn't bear to face Garth, tell him what had to be told. That she was going to stay married to Kevin. There was only one choice for her to make. To say goodbye.

Chapter Twenty-Three

"I can't believe you mean that." Garth's voice was rough. "I can't believe you're going to do this to us. To Megan."

Val knew it was going to be heartbreakingly hard to tell Garth her decision. However, she had not really anticipated the violence of his reaction.

When he arrived at the bus stop to meet her, they simply went into each other's arms. Val closed her eyes, allowing herself the fleeting moment of feeling loved, safe. But only for that one fleeting moment. It was too dangerous. She backed out of Garth's embrace, avoiding the puzzled expression on his face.

"Eileen's keeping Megan overnight. I'll take you home," he said quietly. "I went by earlier, lit a fire. It should be warm by now." He took her small bag, then helped her into the car.

They stepped inside the cottage and Val saw the fire, the bunch of bronze and gold chrysanthemums in a pottery vase on the table. There was something savory simmering on the stove and the sharp fragrance of fresh coffee. She smiled gratefully at Garth. All these thoughtful touches welcoming her home.

Garth moved toward her. She could tell he wanted to take her in his arms again. "So glad you're back. I missed you."

Then before she could stop herself, she blurted out, "Garth, I told Kevin I'd wait for him."

Garth stepped back from her, a look of disappointment and shock on his face. "You don't mean that."

"It's true," Val rushed on. Once she had started, she might as well let it all out. "I talked to both the chaplain and the warden. They both feel it's the only thing that will keep Kevin sane, keep him alive in that place. The hope that there will be something for him when he gets out. Or even sooner. They said he had a good chance of parole and that having me waiting was part of his rehabilitation—"

Garth muttered something under his breath, a combination of swearing or a moan, Val didn't know which. Then he burst out, "I knew that man would talk you into it—play on your principles, make you feel guilty, make you feel responsible. Well, I've got news for them. It isn't your responsibility. Kevin is where he is through his own fault, not yours."

"You don't understand, Garth. Nobody talked me into it."

"Oh, you're so naive, Val. You were taken in for all the years you were married to that guy. You said you had no idea what he was doing. He's clever all right. Now he's counting on your pity." He started to pace, then spun around, fists clenched, and declared, "Well, I won't give you up."

"Garth—"

"No, Val, no! I'm not going to let you do this. Whatever the rationale. I won't let you throw your life away like this. Be a martyr. Make a sacrifice of yourself and of me. I know you love me. No matter what they told you or what they persuaded you to agree with up there. I'm going to fight it."

"Nobody made me do anything, Garth. You must understand—"

"No, I don't have to understand. Why should I? It's my life you're dealing with as well as your own. And Megan's. I love you too much to let you go by default. It doesn't make sense. We—you, Megan and I—we're becoming a family. More than you ever had with Kevin. He forfeited his right to you two years ago. He was the one who wanted the divorce, right? He gave you up. Now, for his own purposes, he wants you back. No, I won't let him do it. He's not going to ruin all our lives."

"Garth, it's my fault. I should have done what Kevin wanted me to in the first place, and I should have told you the truth to begin with. I blame myself for everything."

"That's all in the past, Val. I'm not talking about what's past."

"But don't you see, Garth? It's the past that's the problem. I'm a prisoner of the past."

"You don't have to be a prisoner, Val. That's what I'm trying to get you to see. It's possible for a prisoner to escape."

"But I made promises—"

"Promises under different circumstances. At a different time. Did Kevin keep his promises?" he demanded.

"He deceived you, deprived you, threw you out into the world to fend for yourself. What do you owe him?"

"I'm not talking about that. Maybe you don't understand that I made a new promise. Up there at the prison. I promised Kevin I'd wait and when he got out we'd make a new start."

At last the whole truth was out. Garth seemed instantly sobered by this statement.

"Do you realize he may have to serve his entire sentence?" Garth's voice was harsh, angry. "Do you know how slim his chances for parole are? The wheels of justice turn slowly. There's been a lot of discussion lately about the courts being soft on crime. The public is very aware of this, watching politicians, demanding tougher sentencing, prisoners serving out their complete sentences. Have you considered that you may have promised to wait for a man who will be totally different from the man you knew? A stranger to Megan. An aging man, hardened by prison, his association with fellow prisoners. Have you thought of that beyond some emotional decision, some sentimental ideal that it's your duty?"

"Oh, Garth, don't. I did what I thought was the right thing, the only thing. I couldn't turn my back on Kevin if there was any way I could help. If I deserted him now, I don't know what he'd have to keep going."

"He should have thought of that when he stole all that money," Garth said bitterly.

"How long is he supposed to pay for his mistake?"

"The law has pretty much decided that, hasn't it?" Garth retorted. "But they didn't sentence you, too. Val, why should you be punished? Or Megan? Have you thought of what this is going to do to her? To suddenly have a father after all this time? Are you going to tell her that her father has been in jail? I don't think you've really thought this through."

"Oh, Garth, I have. I've thought of little else for the past few days. Give me credit for that." Val's voice cracked a little. She felt exhausted not only from her journey, but from going over and over all that they were now discussing. "All I know is that Kevin needs me."

"I need you, too," Garth said morosely.

"Not the way Kevin does."

There was a long silence. The only sound was the crackling sizzle in the stove, and the intermittent banging of a shutter somewhere on the house. Garth inclined his head in that direction as if the noise annoyed him. Then he turned back to Val. "Val, you can't give your life like a gift to someone," he said seriously. "Please don't make the mistake of thinking because Kevin tells you he's changed, things will be different when he gets out. You have no more guarantee of that than the possibility of his parole. You may be wasting your youth, your happiness, your life, on a slim chance that he will change." He sighed deeply. "Not just yours, but mine and Megan's, too."

Val put her fingers on her suddenly throbbing temples. "Stop, please, Garth. I've made up my mind. I know what I have to do. There's no use arguing."

In a few strides, Garth was beside her. Holding her shoulders, he turned her to face him. His voice was edged with desperation. "Val, don't do this to us."

Her sobs came then and she covered her face with her hands.

Feeling Garth gently drawing her close, Val pulled away. The urge to let him comfort her was strong but she had to be stronger. For both their sakes. In his embrace, all Val's resolutions would weaken. All her brave words seem meaningless. How much she wanted to allow him to ease her pain, hold her safe. Yet, she couldn't allow it. Not now.

She heard him murmur, "Don't cry, darling. We'll work it out. I promise you, we'll find a way."

She listened, but all the time she knew what path she'd be taking. There was no going back. In Garth's embrace, anything would seem possible. But the irrevocable truth was that she had promised to stay with Kevin "for better for worse" and those vows still bound her.

After a long while, Val's tears were spent. She found some tissues and wiped her eyes.

Nearby, she heard Garth sigh. "You're exhausted. We won't talk anymore tonight. We can't make sense out of anything at this point." He tenderly stroked her hair, then said, "Get a good night's sleep, Val. I'll be over tomorrow morning. We'll figure something out."

Tired as she was, Val had difficulty falling asleep. There was too much on her mind. Things she could not explain to Garth. He had an answer to all her arguments and they were valid. There was one thing he could not answer, nor could anyone else. How could they build their happiness on someone else's misery? The only answer was in Val's own conscience. Whatever anyone said or thought, Val knew what she had to do.

Chapter Twenty-Four

Val woke up, looked at the clock. It was nearly six. The fire had gone out and the house was cold. Shivering, she got up, made coffee. The past three days seemed unreal. Only the inevitableness of what she must do remained clear. She would have to go away. Someplace where Garth wouldn't follow. There had to be a clean break, otherwise...

Val didn't trust herself. If she stayed in Seawood, it was only a matter of time before her resistance would break down. She and Garth were already on thin ice. She had felt it so strongly the night before. From somewhere in her deepest soul, the Scriptural warning came back to her with new, relevant meaning. Matthew 5:28. She and Garth had wanted to do more than just look at each other with desire. She had never before felt tempted. There had never been another man until Garth.

She must get out of harm's way before she was destroyed. She knew her own weakness. It would ruin everything they had together if they took something they weren't free to take. If she divorced Kevin now, she might wipe out any chance he had of getting paroled. If she married Garth, how could she ever forget the price that her longing for happiness would cost Kevin? She just couldn't go through with it. Before that happened, there was only one thing to do. Escape.

Chaplain Scott and the prison counselor had both pointed out to her how her presence and support would work on Kevin's behalf when he came up for parole. It could be the deciding factor. She had given them her word. She couldn't go back on it.

Once, Garth had promised he was willing to continue their relationship on her terms. But they had moved far beyond that first attraction. Their love for each other could no longer be denied. She didn't even trust herself and she loved him too much to expect him to.

Garth's familiar knock on the cottage door startled her. She was even more surprised to see he was wearing a corduroy sport jacket, shirt and tie. He looked haggard, as if he hadn't had much sleep, either.

"Come in, I have coffee made."

He shook his head, held up one hand. "No, thanks, I can't. I'm flying to L.A. today on business. I've been putting it off, but I think I might as well go and get it done. It will give us both a few days to think things through."

Val was taken aback. She had somehow expected that they would spend the day together, talking more. But maybe this was better.

"I just wanted you to know that I love you, Val. I know we can have a wonderful life together. I can't persuade you against your will. But I think—I hope— when you've had time to weigh everything, you'll realize what we have together is worth fighting for. At least,

I'm willing to fight for it. There's so much to gain and everything to lose if…"

He pressed his lips together. She could tell there was more he wanted to say but couldn't decide whether to or not. He glanced away from her, down toward the beach. When he spoke again, his voice was rough with emotion.

"What we can give to Megan is worth more than some promise you made under emotional stress." He stood there for another long minute, then said, "I love you, Val."

"I love you, too," Val replied, thinking, You'll never know how much.

When he was gone, all the tears she had kept back while Garth was there burst out. She wept as if she would never stop. Sobbing, she threw herself on the couch, burying her face in the pillows. Finally, spent and shaken, she lay there thinking, This is the way it feels when your heart is breaking.

It was a physical pain as well as an emotional one. It was then she decided she couldn't wait until Garth returned. It would be too late. She wouldn't have the courage to go. She had to leave now. She got up, stood uncertainly for a few minutes in the middle of the room, wondering what to do first. Of course, she must tell Garth why. Write him a letter. Put it all down in writing so he could not argue her out of it. Yes, that was the best way.

She got out paper and pen, sat down at the kitchen table and began to write.

Dearest Garth,
By the time you read this, I shall be far from here.

Please forgive me for hurting you by doing it like this. I would hurt you far more if I stayed. I love you and I always will. But it's impossible for me to remain here and be true to myself and what I've promised.

I take full responsibility for what has happened. I blame myself for giving you a false impression of my situation when we met. I became tangled in my own web. But as you've said so often, the past is the past, I can't undo anything. I just ask you not to hate me for messing up your life.

I know you don't understand why I can't desert Kevin at this point. I just can't cut the ties that still bind me to him.

I will always be thankful for having known you, proud that you loved me and wanted me. I will be forever grateful for your loving my little girl and becoming a part of our lives. I'm sure she will never forget you.

I could go on and on writing about all the things about you and our time together that I'll remember and cherish for the rest of my life. I will just close now and say God bless you, Garth, and thank you for all you've done for me and been to me.

Goodbye,

Val hesitated before she signed her name. Somehow the words she'd written seemed cold, stiff. And yet to pour out all the deeply felt love she had for him, the things she might have whispered in his arms, would only hurt him more. Quickly, she folded the letter, slipped it in an envelope. She would put it in his mailbox when she went up to the McDermotts' for Megan.

She packed Megan's clothes and her own, ironically in the same four suitcases she had brought with her that night two years before. She had not acquired many new things and only replaced clothes that Megan had outgrown.

She then took out the strongbox in which she kept her cash. She had never opened an account at the local bank because of all the information that had to be put on an application. In a way that was lucky. There would be no unnecessary delay. She counted it out. She had accumulated a good sum in all these months. There was enough for bus fare to San Francisco—from there she could decide where to go—and enough to live on for a few weeks until she got settled, found a job. She was trembling with nerves by the time she got everything together. She took one long, last look around the little cottage that had been their home, that had held so many times of happiness as well as of sorrow. Now they were off again, like two Gypsies, to find another place to hide for who knew how long.

Of course, Eileen tried to dissuade Val from going.

"Don't be a fool, Val! Don't turn your back on a man like Garth, a chance for real happiness. I've been around a lot longer than you have and I know you two have something special. Think what this will do to him. And what about Megan? She loves Garth. Please, listen to me, Val. Believe me, if you do this, you'll regret it."

"Eileen, I have to go. I've thought of it from every possible angle. This way, we'll get over the hurt faster.

If I stayed, we'd both be dying by inches knowing that eventually I had to keep my promise to Kevin. Don't you understand?"

Eileen sighed. "Maybe you're right. But where are you going, where will you be?"

"I don't know for sure, Eileen. Besides, I can't tell you. That way, you won't have to lie to Garth if he tries to find out. And he mustn't find out, Eileen. One thing you've got to promise me, that if I use The Seawinds and you and Tom as a reference for another job, you won't tell Garth. Promise?"

Reluctantly, Eileen agreed. Her eyes welled with tears as she helped Megan get dressed while Val called a cab to take them to the bus station in Oceanview. Eileen hugged them both hard and, at the last minute, stuffed a wad of bills into Val's hand.

The taxi honked, and after another quick hug, Val grabbed their suitcases and they ran out to the waiting car, through a light rain. As the cab made the turn onto the highway, Val took a last look back at the rustic restaurant building and then down to the gray beach, the crashing breakers, the wheeling seagulls, until they all were enveloped in mist. Then she turned and, for the rest of the ride, stared straight ahead.

At the bus station, Val went to the ticket counter and determinedly purchased two one-way tickets to San Francisco.

Megan didn't grasp the full impact of what they were doing. Val knew she would have a great deal of explaining to do later on. For now, Megan was happy as they boarded the bus, ready for a new adventure.

It wasn't until they were on their way that Val took

the money Eileen had pressed on her out of her wallet and saw six fifty-dollar bills. Val nearly broke down then and there. She was leaving not only the man she loved but the dearest, kindest friends she had ever known. Would she ever be that happy again, anywhere?

PART III

Chapter Twenty-Five

When word came from the prison that Kevin's parole had been granted, Val found herself emotionally unprepared. Although it had been a possibility for the past ten months, the news still came with an unexpected suddenness.

The call had come on Monday from Chaplain Scott saying that Kevin would be released at noon the next Friday. Could she come to the prison to pick him up?

"Of course," Val had replied through stiff lips. When she replaced the receiver of the kitchen wall phone, she slumped weakly against the sink, gripping the metal edge of the counter to steady herself.

"It's too soon," she thought irrationally. *I'm not ready.* Not ready to begin life again with a man from whom she'd been separated for almost three years, a man she had tried to put out of her heart and mind, a man she wasn't even sure she still loved.

Quickly she reminded herself that it wasn't too soon for Kevin. He'd been increasingly impatient every month when she'd gone to see him. He'd been irritable, nervous, constantly cracking his knuckles in clenched hands. She'd leave after a visit, feeling uneasy, upset. She tried to explain away Kevin's snappishness with her. She was reminded of all the other times when he'd lashed out at her. Become angry over some small incident or something she'd failed to do. Kev had a short fuse, always had. And, of course, he was under severe tension. It was understandable, she told herself.

She looked around the sunny kitchen trying to make sense of the phone call. It seemed to come from some faraway, foreign place. Far removed from the peaceful life she'd found in Spring Valley. This small northern California town, deep in Redwood Country, was where she and Megan now lived. Coming here had been happenstance.

It had been a last-minute decision, actually. After heartbrokenly leaving Seawood, Val had been uncertain about the best place for her and Megan to go. Living in a city would be expensive and finding a safe area to live, reliable sitters for Megan when she was at work, would be difficult. So when they reached San Francisco, Val extended their ticket farther north. It would be a greater distance from Seawood but closer to the prison situated on the Oregon border.

That decision had been a good one. They'd found a nice duplex at reasonable rent and within walking distance to school for Megan. Val had found two part-time jobs, one during Megan's school hours, the other a billing job she could do from home for a local catalog company. They had joined a church and Megan had made many friends and was happy.

Now with Kevin coming back into their lives, everything would change. Once more Val thought, *It's too soon.* The thing that terrified her was this, was it too late for her and Kevin to build a life together?

The rest of the week went by with frightening swiftness. As Val hurried around getting everything in readiness, she felt time was rushing by, hurtling her forward into an unknown future.

Mrs. Ellerbee, the fiftyish widow, who lived on the other side of Val's apartment, was more than willing to keep Megan. She had become a friend and confidante in the months Val had lived next door. She had grandchildren who sometimes visited her on weekends and Megan was perfectly comfortable with the arrangement. In the past months, little by little, Val had talked to Megan about her father, told her that he might be coming home to live with them again. With a child's astonishing flexibility, Megan seemed to accept that without a qualm. The fact that he would be home in a few days seemed only natural.

Val wished she had the same attitude. The closer Friday approached, the more inner turmoil she felt. She couldn't sleep, or eat. Then at last it was Friday.

Val's hands gripped the steering wheel of the secondhand compact she had bought a few months before. Merging into the flow of traffic on the freeway, Val's heart pumped wildly. She slid in a tape hoping some of the Amy Grant songs Megan loved and had learned to sing would be calming. It was a bright, beautiful spring morning and she knew she should be feeling happy. Yet a thousand doubts clouded her mind. She remembered the last conversation she'd had with Chaplain Scott on one of her recent visits to Kevin. He'd been waiting for her and asked her to come into his office.

"I know Kevin thinks his parole is a done deal," he'd told her, "and his optimism is better than the depression he went through. But it's never a certainty, although his chances are immeasurably improved by your standing by him. I just don't want to hold out any false hope that if and when he gets out, everything's going to be perfect, that you will live happily ever after. Unfortunately, it's been my experience that even if an ex-convict is lucky enough to find a job, many of them get restless in a routine, ordinary situation. The everyday life that they've fantasized about in prison begins to look pretty dull. That's when some find it hard to resist the temptation to look for the easy money they may have found in illegal ways...the very things that landed them in prison. I hope this won't be the case with your husband."

Strangely enough, the chaplain's caution had come right on top of that day's visit. Kevin had been talking enthusiastically about the correspondence course he had enrolled in by mail.

"Real estate is where the big money is these days. There's a regular gold mine in land investment and development. The second-home trend is really booming. There are a lot of people in big jobs making huge salaries that take early retirement and want to get out of the big cities, want homes in scenic environments, out of the rat race and urban problems. Northern California and Oregon are ripe for this game."

Val had not thought much about that since. But somehow recalling the chaplain's warning coupled with the memory of Kevin's enthusiasm made her a little uneasy. Instinctively, she had a hunch that Kevin wouldn't be satisfied with a salesclerk's job at a department store such as the ones Val saw advertised in the local paper.

She parked her car several yards from the prison in sight of the guardhouse and gate. Her hands were sweaty and she had to keep wiping them with tissues. This was it. The end of the endless waiting. Calm down, calm down, Val ordered herself. The strain was like a wire pulled excruciatingly tight. It was hard to breathe. The shriek of the prison's noon whistle split the air. Val tensed, eyes riveted on the prison gate.

Then she saw it open and a man stepped out through the narrow doorway in the heavy steel gate. She pushed open the car door and got out. She waved. "Kevin! Over here, Kevin!"

Kevin put the six-pack in the refrigerator, let the door slam. He pulled the metal tab on one can with a swishing sound. Then he swung one of the kitchen chairs out from the table, turned it around, straddled it. Leaning his arms on its back, he took a swallow of beer, then looked around.

"Believe me, baby, I'll soon have us out of this dump."

Val swallowed back an indignant retort. Kevin had only been out a week, but he'd found fault with everything in the little duplex she had worked so hard to spruce up for him. The fresh café curtains, the row of African violets blooming on the windowsill, the framed Renoir prints on the freshly painted walls, the new bedspread in the bedroom they now shared. Everything had been scrubbed and polished to a gleaming shine.

It will take time, Val reminded herself. But trying to

heed the chaplain's advice was difficult. She had been on her own for a long time. Now Kevin was back, running the show like in the old days before anything had happened to change things. She had tried to remain calm, cheerful, but it wasn't easy.

"Do you have a credit card?" he asked. "I can't apply for one yet. But I need to get some new clothes. Gotta look sharp. Image is everything." He took another swig of his beer.

Val picked up her handbag, got out her wallet, took the credit card and handed it over to Kevin.

"What's the credit limit?" he asked.

She told him. She felt guilty that she was reluctant to let him use it. She always paid off the balance every month, so no interest charges had accrued to make the payments too large. She had used it only to get new mattresses for the beds, a microwave and a small TV when they first moved into the duplex. But Kevin was probably planning to go on job interviews now that he had had a chance to get settled. Just being out of prison was a big adjustment.

"Have you some interviews lined up?"

It seemed a reasonable question. She wasn't prepared for Kevin's explosion.

"Stop nagging, will you? I'm not going to line up at some employment office, if that's what you mean. I've got my own plans. Big ones."

Val was startled at his reaction. There hadn't been any justification for his angry response. Soon after that, Kevin took the car keys and left.

He came back late. Val had already fed Megan her supper and was in the kitchen washing up when he returned. He was loaded with packages and bags bearing the logo of a well-known men's clothing store. He was wearing a striped shirt, raw-silk sport coat, Italian loafers. He looked like the old Kevin. "Wow!" was all Val could say.

Kevin was obviously pleased with himself. He went into the bedroom and Val heard dresser drawers being opened, the closet door being pushed back. Kevin was evidently putting all his new purchases away. Val could only imagine what her credit-card bill would list when it arrived at the first of next month.

She tried not to feel resentful. Kevin needed the boost of self-confidence some good-looking clothes would give him. His self-esteem had been ground down to zero in prison. Buying all these expensive clothes could be considered part of the expense of his rehabilitation. Probably it was well worth it.

A few days later, Kevin announced that he was going to drive to San Francisco to meet a friend, a business associate.

"Someone I know?" Val asked, wondering if Kevin had been in touch with any of his former colleagues at the bank.

"No." He sounded sullen. "If you must know, it's a guy I met in prison." Val's shock must have shown because Kevin snarled, "Don't give me that sanctimonious look. It doesn't mean he was in for murder. White-collar crime, remember? Jerry had a run-in with the IRS, some tax problem, that's all. But he's a sharp fellow. He can put me in touch with some of the people I need to connect with in real estate."

They were in the kitchen, and Megan, dressed and

ready for school, came in just then and said, "Mommy, I need my lunch."

Kevin said, "Don't interrupt, Megan. Your mother and I are having a conversation." Val saw at once that Megan hadn't heard him, for she went on talking. Kevin evidently didn't realize that and yanked the little girl by her shoulder, turning her toward him. "I said don't interrupt."

Megan looked frightened, bewildered. "I'm sorry, Daddy."

"Kevin," Val protested, tapping her ear with her forefinger in an attempt to explain.

Kevin gave her an irritated glance and demanded, "What?"

"I'll tell you later," she said, and handed Megan her lunchbox, leaned down and kissed her, then took her by the hand and saw her out the door. Returning to the kitchen, she managed to say in a calm voice, "Kevin, Megan didn't mean to interrupt. She didn't hear us talking when she came in."

Kevin scowled. "Is she worse? Maybe we should investigate a school where she'd be with other handicapped kids."

"Handicapped? Megan isn't disabled, Kevin!" Val struggled not to lose her temper. She kept her voice even. "She gets along perfectly well where she is. Her teachers are very complimentary about how attentive she is, how well she participates—"

"Okay, okay. End of discussion." Kevin pushed back his chair, slammed his coffee mug down on the table, then stood up. "I've got to get going. I'm renting a car. A new model. Can't be seen driving a clunker. You'll have to go with me to the car rental, sign it out for me. I don't want to fill out an application for one while I'm on parole."

Upset at how he had treated Megan, Val said, "Kevin, we have to talk. About Megan."

"Not now, Val. I haven't time." With that, Kevin walked out of the room, leaving Val smoldering. They would have to talk. She started to clear the table. Indeed, there were a great many things they had to talk about.

Kevin picked out a long, sleek, luxury rental car and Val, against her better judgment, signed for it.

Kevin had said he might stay overnight in San Francisco in case the talks went late or Jerry wanted to take him to meet someone. Val was still upset about the scene that morning and did not comment. As she drove her own car back home, she thought this adjustment to living together again was far harder than she had anticipated.

Kevin was jumpy and on edge most of the time. He watched TV with his finger constantly on the remote, switching channels as if nothing could hold his attention. His sleep was disturbed with nightmares. He would wake up often, then take a pillow and blanket and spend the remainder of the night on the living-room couch. After their first night together, which turned out to be a failure, they had not regained the physical intimacy that had been such a big part of their relationship before. His relationship with Megan, for which she had such high hopes, was also disappointing. After an initial rush of excitement, Kevin resumed his distracted, indifferent attitude toward her. He seemed annoyed by her deafness, which he seemed to have forgotten about.

More and more, Val wondered if she had done the right thing. More and more, her thoughts returned to Garth. What had he done when he read her letter? Where was he now? It was useless to go over and over it all again. She had done what she thought was right at the time. It had to work. She had to try harder. "Dear God, help me," she whispered.

When she met Jerry Meisner, Val thought, *I don't like him.* There was something about him that made her recoil. He was too smooth, too quick with a compliment, his laugh too forced, his smile phony. Something about his eyes… Val disliked being so critical of the man Kevin had introduced her to at the airport. But there it was. She couldn't help it. Kevin was excited, up. Val hadn't seen him so positive and confident since he'd gotten out of prison. There was the old spring in his step, the ready wit and spontaneous enthusiasm. No wonder Meisner's associates wanted someone like Kevin as their sales representative.

They were flying to Lake Tahoe for a big bash, a party to be held at the model home Meisner's construction company had built—one of the many they hoped to build and sell on lakeside sites. It was going to be a grand affair—food and wine and sales talk. Kevin would be in his element.

Val had mixed feelings as he gave her a quick hug and kiss before the two men, still talking, walked into the terminal to board the company's private Cessna. Kevin glanced over his shoulder once and, seeing Val still standing there, gave her a jaunty wave.

* * *

That night, Val and Megan had supper alone, and Val sat on Megan's bed to read her a story. "This is nice, isn't it, Mommy? Just you and me," Megan said as she cuddled close. Val hugged her. She knew Megan was sensitive to the tension that Kevin's presence made in their little house, where once it had been so cozy and relaxed.

Val settled Megan down for the night, then took a long bath and went to bed. She wondered how the party at Lake Tahoe was going and if Kevin had made any sales. If he was successful, would he want them to move to Tahoe? What did the future hold for them? Before anything was decided, she had to talk to Kevin about Megan. Their little girl was eight now and they would have to make some plans if her deafness was increasing.

After her bath, Val was too tired to watch TV. Instead, she read for a while, then went to sleep.

The persistent peal of her doorbell brought Val awake. A glance at the bedside clock told her it was nearly six. Had Kevin come back already? Forgotten his key? She grabbed her robe, flung it around her shoulders and ran barefoot to the front door.

Somehow she knew, even before anything was said, when she opened the door and saw the two highway patrolmen, tall and erect in their crisp uniforms, standing on the steps.

A private plane with four passengers had crashed upon takeoff from the Tahoe airport. Kevin was one of the passengers. They were sorry to inform her that there were no survivors.

Chapter Twenty-Six

The summer Megan was ten, Val made arrangements for her to attend Girl Scout camp in the Santa Cruz Mountains. Even though she would miss her terribly, Val knew it was important for Megan to become more independent. Happy and excited as she was to go, at the last minute, right before boarding the camp bus, Megan ran back to give her mother one more hug.

In the years since Kevin's death, Val had tried not to be overprotective of the little girl or allow her to become too attached. Especially because of Megan's deafness, Val knew it was important for her to be exposed to different experiences.

Val had taken some accrued vacation days to get Megan ready for camp. She was in no hurry to go back to their duplex, which would seem empty with Megan away. So after seeing her daughter off, Val decided to drive to Carmel. The picturesque little town with its art galleries, boutiques and quaint shops was only a little farther down the coast.

After finding a parking spot, Val strolled leisurely along the winding streets whose sidewalks meandered around trees that gave a leafy shade. The display window in every store she passed offered something to make her take a look and decide whether to go inside or not. However, it was a sign outside one small gallery that brought her to an abrupt halt. It read New Paintings By Garth Hasten.

As she stood there staring at the name, the world seemed to stop turning. Though she was unable to move, her feet rooted to the pavement, her pulse pounded, her heart raced. Was he here? Should she go inside or turn around now and leave?

Finally, curiosity won over hesitation and Val walked inside. Garth was one of several artists exhibited in this gallery. Familiar as she was with his technique, she recognized his at once. Representational, yet there was something new, a freer style, as if influenced by the French Impressionists. The scenes of country landscapes and villages convinced her that he must have gone to France after all. Without them. Val thought of the happy plans he'd made that day by the ocean. Plans that had disappeared like a drift of fog.

There were eight paintings in all signed by GH, but no paintings from the sketches Val knew he had made on the beach when the three of them were all there together. He'd made dozens of sketches of Megan, hoping to use them someday in a picture book with the seashore as background. Megan in her skimpy pink bathing suit she had long since outgrown, standing in the foamy shallows, stooping to examine tide pools, kneeling in the sand, industriously creating her towered castles. What had he done with them?

"May I help you in any way, madam? Are you interested in any of these paintings?"

Val slowly came back to the present at the sound of the question. She turned to see an exotic young woman wearing dangling silver earrings and a black-and-gold leopard-patterned dress regarding her curiously. The gallery manager, she guessed.

"Are you familiar with the artist's work?"

"No, not exactly. I mean, yes, I admire his work. But I'm afraid I couldn't afford any of his paintings."

"He's really quite remarkable in that he's primarily an illustrator of children's books. Few artists make that transition to fine art, but Garth Hasten has. His paintings are much in demand." She gestured to the ones in front of them. "Most of these are sold. See the small red dots in the corners? We had an opening for him earlier in the summer when he was down here. It was very successful."

"I'm glad to hear it."

"We could sell everything he paints. But there are some he's reluctant to part with. In fact, we have two he wouldn't let us put up for this show unless we put NFS stickers on them."

Something made Val ask, "May I see them?"

The young woman hesitated. She seemed to be making a mental calculation. If this wasn't a serious buyer, why was she interested and should she take the time with her? Of course, one never knew. Even with her experience with art collectors, she was sometimes wrong. She glanced around the gallery. There was no one else wandering through at the moment. It had been a slow afternoon. So she said to Val, "Certainly, come this way. We hung them in the annex so that only the most ardent fans of his would seek them out. Especially since he refuses to sell them, it doesn't seem practical for us to display them in the front of the gallery."

The two paintings struck Val's heart with an impact she couldn't have anticipated. One was a long view of a curved beach and walking along the edge were two figures, one of a woman, the other of a little girl. Even though the figures were viewed from behind, Val knew they were of her and Megan. The other one was of a child bent over, holding a seashell in one cupped hand against the background of the ocean, the frothy scallops of water swirling around her small, bare brown feet. There was no doubt. It was Megan at six years of age.

Memories crowded in, making her almost weak with regret. She managed to ask in a husky voice, "Does Mr. Hasten live in Carmel?"

"No. I'm not sure where he lives. He's rather reclusive. I know the gallery owner had to go through his agent to persuade him to do this exhibit. He must travel a good deal. All these current paintings are from a year he spent in France."

Val moved away. She was afraid the young woman would notice the tears that gathered in her eyes.

"Would you like to sign our visitors' book. Be on our mailing list?"

"No, thank you."

"Please take one of our brochures."

Val picked one up off the table at the entrance as she went back outside again. She walked down to the next corner to an outdoor café. She sat at an umbrel-

laed table, ordered a caffe latte and opened the colorful brochure.

"Garth Hasten, well-known illustrator of children's
books, has long been hailed as a fine artist. The current exhibit is a collection from paintings he did while
spending a 'vagabond' year traveling in France."

A tightness formed in Val's throat as she read. Those
were the months that were to have been their honeymoon. She tried to imagine what that time had been
like for Garth. Overall, the paintings had been light,
filled with sunshine, flowers, arbors and cottages, old
stone churches and rolling hills. There was no hint of
melancholy or unhappiness in the artist who painted
them. A spontaneous prayer welled up in Val's heart
for Garth, blessing him.

As she had done daily since they parted, she prayed
that the wounds she'd inflicted on Garth had healed,
that he had forgiven her and not blamed her for what
she had done.

Val left Carmel and started north again. Back on
the freeway, seeing the sign, on impulse she took the
Seawood turnoff. She wasn't sure why. She'd learned
the McDermotts had closed The Seawinds and retired
for good to Mexico. She had written them once, a brief
note after she and Megan were settled, but had put no
return address on the envelope. Since she didn't have
their Mexican address, she hadn't been able to let them
know about Kevin's death. She was sure they had also
lost track of Garth.

The little town of Seawood looked deserted, not
much different from the first time she'd seen it. Progress had passed it by. The businesses that had held on

precariously while The Seawinds was open had closed up shop, probably moved into Oceanview, twenty miles away.

Val drove down the rutted beach road and parked above the cottage that had been her and Megan's home for nearly two years. It looked more weathered and forlorn. Its roof sagged, the rain gutters rusted and bent. Not a sign of life anywhere. Drawn by some unknown pull, Val got out of the car. The day had darkened since she left Carmel. Here, clouds hung ominously over a steel gray choppy ocean. The entire stretch of beach looked abandoned. Didn't even summer people seeking a cheap place to vacation come here anymore?

She had a strange feeling of déjà vu. It was just such a day when she had first arrived here herself. She remembered her dismay at seeing the cottage she had rented. How she had dreaded starting a new life in such a place. And yet she had come to love it. Even on a day like this, the sea, the beach, held a beauty, a fascination for her. She had eventually been happier here than any other place in her life.

Scattered wisps of fog blew up from the ocean. Val breathed deeply of the tangy salt air. She walked down the warped wooden path onto the dunes and then to the beach. There she slipped off her flats and stockings, tucked them in the pocket of her jacket and walked down along the beach to the water's edge. She felt the delicious sensation as the water curled up in between her toes and she dug her feet into the wet sand. She began walking. Gradually, the feelings of calm and peace the ocean had always brought to her soul began to come over her. Oh, how she had missed it all, the smell and sight and feel of the air, sea, sand. She experienced a lightness of heart as she went on, the sensation of a homecoming after a long time away. It seemed so right to be here. She wondered again if God had brought her here the first time and now, had drawn her back.

She stopped to look out at the ocean and saw two solitary surfers in wet suits riding the waves. She stood there long after the surfers had beached, raised their boards over their heads and started walking down the sand in the opposite direction.

Had they found our old cove? Our special place? Val wondered. Would they build a driftwood fire in the shelter of the dunes? Were they lovers? Would they wait for the moon to rise and look into the firelight and dream their dreams—the way she and Garth had once done?

Val walked on, more slowly now, remembering the past, the golden days of the second spring she had lived at Seawood. Then suddenly, she became conscious of a tingling along her spine, a quiver of awareness that she was no longer alone on the beach. She turned away from the ocean and looked up.

On the cliff above, outlined against the gray sky, was a man's figure. Something looked familiar about the set of the head and shoulders. She felt a clutching sensation in her heart. Could it be? Was it possible? As she stood there watching, he made his way down onto the beach. He was striding toward her purposefully. Then he broke into a run and there was no mistake. She knew who it was.

Yet when he was a few feet away, she heard herself say, "I don't believe it."

Even as he came closer, she felt that she must be

dreaming. Then he smiled and said, "I've just made coffee. Will you come up and have some?"

The invitation was a replay of a dozen other times as well as the dialogue in a hundred dreams come true.

"This can't really be happening," she said again when at last they were seated opposite each other in the window of Garth's cottage. "I never thought you'd still be here."

"I couldn't bring myself to leave. Somehow I thought, hoped, prayed, that someday you'd return. So I come down here for a few weeks, try to paint—"

"I've just seen your new paintings in the gallery in Carmel."

"The ones I did in France?"

"Yes, and…the others."

She noticed a subtle change in his expression, then Garth reached across for her left hand, lifted it and examined her fourth finger. "No wedding ring? You didn't go back to your husband after all?"

"Kevin's dead, Garth." Garth's eyebrows lifted. Skeptically? Val realized he was considering the lie she had told him before, the one that had caused them both such pain. She felt ashamed, remembering. "This time it's true."

Quickly, Val explained the circumstances of Kevin's parole and what had happened to him.

"How long ago?"

"Two years."

"Then why…?" Garth frowned, letting his unspoken question hang between them. "Why didn't you get in touch with me?" he finally asked.

"I'm not sure. Maybe because I was afraid I had hurt

you too much. That you were well rid of me. I thought you must have met someone else by then, maybe even married. Besides, you had gone to France—"

"I would have come back. Don't you know that, Val? If I'd known, nothing would have kept me from coming." Garth's hold on her hand tightened. "I've never stopped loving you, Val. I can't tell you how empty my life has been without you and Megan."

It seemed incredible to Val. That those long, lonely years had ended with this remarkable reunion. She could still hardly believe it was real until he had gathered her into his arms…until she felt the warmth of his lips on hers as she welcomed his kiss.

"My darling," Val heard Garth's voice say over and over as he held her close. There would be time, she knew, when all this could be explained, when all the pieces of the scattered puzzle would be picked up, examined, reexamined and put together at last. There was so much to tell, so much time to make up for, but they had all the time in the world. They had forever.

Together they went to pick Megan up from camp. When the little girl saw Garth, there was hardly a moment's hesitation before she ran and flung herself into his outstretched arms.

He swung her around, then set her down, and she turned happily to Val, saying, "Oh, Mom, where did you find him?" They all laughed, and as Val's gaze met Garth's over Megan's head, she knew that at last she had found the man who would share with her all the joys, responsibilities and struggles of raising a child. A man she could trust and love.

She had been alone so long. And now she was being given a second chance. A second chance for a new life, a new love.

In September at the Wayside Chapel, a small church set deep among the redwoods, Val and Garth were married. It seemed the appropriate and the perfect place for a wedding. Polished beams of glowing wood overhead led to the altar behind which were three arched windows overlooking a beautiful valley. Through the glass, two stately redwood trees rose side by side, soaring into the sky. Above the altar on a cross beam were carved the words, "Faith, Hope and Love and the greatest of these is Love."

As she and Garth joined hands to repeat their pledges, Val knew that these spiritual principles would guide and direct their life together, strengthening their commitment to each other in the sacred promises they would keep forever.

* * * * *

REQUEST YOUR FREE BOOKS!

2 FREE INSPIRATIONAL NOVELS
PLUS 2
FREE
MYSTERY GIFTS

Love Inspired

REQUEST YOUR FREE BOOKS!

2 FREE INSPIRATIONAL NOVELS
PLUS 2
FREE
MYSTERY GIFTS

Love Inspired
HISTORICAL
INSPIRATIONAL HISTORICAL ROMANCE

YES! Please send me 2 FREE Love Inspired® Historical novels and my 2 FREE mystery gifts (gifts are worth about $10). After receiving them, if I don't wish to receive any more books, I can return the shipping statement marked "cancel." If I don't cancel, I will receive 4 brand-new novels every month and be billed just $4.49 per book in the U.S. or $4.99 per book in Canada. That's a savings of at least 22% off the cover price. It's quite a bargain! Shipping and handling is just 50¢ per book in the U.S. and 75¢ per book in Canada.* I understand that accepting the 2 free books and gifts places me under no obligation to buy anything. I can always return a shipment and cancel at any time. Even if I never buy another book, the two free books and gifts are mine to keep forever.

102/302 IDN FV2V

Name	(PLEASE PRINT)	
Address		Apt. #
City	State/Prov.	Zip/Postal Code

Signature (if under 18, a parent or guardian must sign)

Mail to the **Harlequin® Reader Service:**
IN U.S.A.: P.O. Box 1867, Buffalo, NY 14240-1867
IN CANADA: P.O. Box 609, Fort Erie, Ontario L2A 5X3

Want to try two free books from another series?
Call 1-800-873-8635 or visit www.ReaderService.com.

* Terms and prices subject to change without notice. Prices do not include applicable taxes. Sales tax applicable in N.Y. Canadian residents will be charged applicable taxes. Offer not valid in Quebec. This offer is limited to one order per household. Not valid for current subscribers to Love Inspired Historical books. All orders subject to credit approval. Credit or debit balances in a customer's account(s) may be offset by any other outstanding balance owed by or to the customer. Please allow 4 to 6 weeks for delivery. Offer available while quantities last.

Your Privacy—The Harlequin® Reader Service is committed to protecting your privacy. Our Privacy Policy is available online at www.ReaderService.com or upon request from the Harlequin Reader Service.

We make a portion of our mailing list available to reputable third parties that offer products we believe may interest you. If you prefer that we not exchange your name with third parties, or if you wish to clarify or modify your communication preferences, please visit us at www.ReaderService.com/consumerschoice or write to us at Harlequin Reader Service Preference Service, P.O. Box 9062, Buffalo, NY 14269. Include your complete name and address.

LIHDIR13

REQUEST YOUR FREE BOOKS!

2 FREE RIVETING INSPIRATIONAL NOVELS
PLUS 2 FREE MYSTERY GIFTS

YES! Please send me 2 FREE Love Inspired® Suspense novels and my 2 FREE mystery gifts (gifts are worth about $10). After receiving them, if I don't wish to receive any more books, I can return the shipping statement marked "cancel." If I don't cancel, I will receive 4 brand-new novels every month and be billed just $4.49 per book in the U.S. or $4.99 per book in Canada. That's a savings of at least 22% off the cover price. It's quite a bargain! Shipping and handling is just 50¢ per book in the U.S. and 75¢ per book in Canada.* I understand that accepting the 2 free books and gifts places me under no obligation to buy anything. I can always return a shipment and cancel at any time. Even if I never buy another book, the two free books and gifts are mine to keep forever.

123/323 IDN FVZV

Name _____ (PLEASE PRINT) _____

Address _____ Apt. # _____

City _____ State/Prov. _____ Zip/Postal Code _____

Signature (if under 18, a parent or guardian must sign) _____

Mail to the Harlequin® Reader Service:
IN U.S.A.: P.O. Box 1867, Buffalo, NY 14240-1867
IN CANADA: P.O. Box 609, Fort Erie, Ontario L2A 5X3

**Are you a subscriber to Love Inspired Suspense
and want to receive the larger-print edition?
Call 1-800-873-8635 or visit www.ReaderService.com.**

* Terms and prices subject to change without notice. Prices do not include applicable taxes. Sales tax applicable in N.Y. Canadian residents will be charged applicable taxes. Offer not valid in Quebec. This offer is limited to one order per household. Not valid for current subscribers to Love Inspired Suspense books. All orders subject to credit approval. Credit or debit balances in a customer's account(s) may be offset by any other outstanding balance owed by or to the customer. Please allow 4 to 6 weeks for delivery. Offer available while quantities last.

Your Privacy—The Harlequin® Reader Service is committed to protecting your privacy. Our Privacy Policy is available online at www.ReaderService.com or upon request from the Harlequin Reader Service.
We make a portion of our mailing list available to reputable third parties that offer products we believe may interest you. If you prefer that we not exchange your name with third parties, or if you wish to clarify or modify your communication preferences, please visit us at www.ReaderService.com/consumerschoice or write to us at Harlequin Reader Service Preference Service, P.O. Box 9062, Buffalo, NY 14269. Include your complete name and address.